Praise for Paul Kane

'Paul Kane is a first-rate storyteller, never failing to marry his insights into the world and its anguish with the pleasures of phrases eloquently turned.'

(**Clive Barker** — Bestselling author of *The Hellbound Heart, Abarat, Mr B. Gone & The Scarlet Gospels*)

'Paul Kane's lean, stripped-back prose is a tool that's very much fit for purpose. He knows how to make you want to avoid the shadows and the cracks in the pavement.'

(**Mike Carey** — Bestselling author of the Felix Castor series of novels and *The Girl With All the Gifts, Fellside* and *The Boy on the Bridge* as M.R. Carey)

'Kane finds the everyday horrors buried within us, rips them out and serves them up in these deliciously dark tales.'

(**Kelley Armstrong** — Bestselling author of *Bitten, Haunted, Broken, Waking the Witch, Spell Bound* and *Thirteen*)

'I'm impressed by the range of Paul Kane's imagination. It seems there is no risk, no high-stakes gamble, he fears to take…Kane's foot never gets even close to the brake pedal.'

(**Peter Straub** — Bestselling author of *Ghost Story, Mr X, Lost Boy Lost Girl*, and *In the Night Room*)

'Paul Kane is a name to watch. His work is disturbing and very creepy.'

(**Tim Lebbon** — New York Times bestselling author of *The Cabin in the Woods, The Silence* and *Relics*)

'His stories not only, at his best, put him neck and neck with Ramsey Campbell and Clive Barker, but also in the company of greats like Machen and MR James. You don't rest easily after reading a Paul Kane story, but strangely your eyes have been somewhat opened.'

(Stephen Volk — BAFTA winning screenwriter of *Gothic*, *Ghostwatch*, *Afterlife*, *The Awakening* and *Midwinter of the Spirit*; author of *Whitstable*, *Leytonstone* and *The Parts We Play*)

'He stands out as one of the better writers I've read.'

(*Eternal Night*)

'Wonderfully dark and satisfying.'

(*Dark Side Magazine*)

'Kane is best when taking risks with his bizarre flights of imagination.'

(*SFX Magazine*)

'Kane is a highly regarded author whose influence can be felt across the genre, with a large and notable body of work behind him.'

(*Starburst Magazine*)

Paul Kane

The Controllers

First published by Luna Press Publishing, Edinburgh, 2019

Astral. *First Published in The Dream Zone, Issue 2 April 1999.*
Eye of the Beholder. *First Published in Alone (In the Dark), BJM 2001.*
Pain Cages. *First Published in Pain Cages, Books of the Dead 2011.*
Secrets. *First Published as 'The Controllers', in Disexistence, Cycatrix Press 2017.*
The Scoop (original to this collection)
Reflections (original to this collection)
They Watch. *First Published in Cemetery Poets: Grave Offerings, Double Dragon Books, 2003.*

www.lunapresspublishing.com
ISBN-13: 978-1-911143-69-7

For Pete Atkins, excellent mate and fellow traveller.

Other Books by Paul Kane:

Novels
Arrowhead
Broken Arrow
Arrowland
Hooded Man (Omnibus)
The Gemini Factor
Of Darkness and Light
Lunar
Sleeper(s)
The Rainbow Man (as P.B. Kane)
Blood RED
Sherlock Holmes and the Servants of Hell
Before
Deep RED

Novellas & Novelettes
Signs of Life
The Lazarus Condition
Dalton Quayle Rides Out
RED
Pain Cages
Creakers (chapbook)
Flaming Arrow
The Bric-a-Brac Man
The P.I.'s Tale
Snow
The Rot
Beneath the Surface (with Simon Clark)

Collections
Alone (In the Dark)
Touching the Flame
FunnyBones
Peripheral Visions

The Adventures of Dalton Quayle
Shadow Writer
The Butterfly Man and Other Stories
The Spaces Between
Ghosts
Monsters
The Dead Trilogy
The Spirits of Christmas
Shadow Casting
Nailbiters
Death
The Life Cycle
Disexistence
Kane's Scary Tales
More Monsters
Lost Souls
Forthcoming: Traumas

Editor & Co-Editor
Shadow Writers Vol. 1 & 2
Terror Tales #1-4
Top International Horror
Albions Alptraume: Zombies
The British Fantasy Society: A Celebration
Hellbound Hearts
The Mammoth Book of Body Horror
A Carnivàle of Horror: Dark Tales from the Fairground
Beyond Rue Morgue
Dark Mirages

Non-Fiction
Contemporary North American Film Directors: A Wallflower
Critical Guide (Major Contributor)
Cinema Macabre (Contributor)
The Hellraiser Films And Their Legacy

Voices in the Dark
Shadow Writer—The Non-Fiction. Vol. 1: Reviews
Shadow Writer—The Non-Fiction. Vol. 2: Articles & Essays
Leviathan—The Story of Hellraiser and Hellbound: Hellraiser
II (contributor)
Hellraisers

Acknowledgments:

My thanks to Francesca and Rob at Luna for being willing to go on this wild ride with me. A huge thank you to Richard Christian Matheson for the amazing introduction and to Ben Baldwin who, once again, has delivered the goods for the cover art. Similarly, thank you to those talented artists who contributed to the gallery you'll find in the extras section of this book, namely: Steve Lines; Daniele Serra; Zach McCain; Paul Bonner Jnr; Anthony Galatis; and Greg Chapman. Delighted the writing inspired such wonderful imagery! As usual, big bear-hugs and massive 'can't thank you enoughs' to all my friends in the writing and film/TV world, for their continual help and support. A very special thank you, though, to people like Clive Barker, Neil Gaiman, Stephen Volk, Mandy Slater, Stephen Jones, Amanda Foubister, Tim Lebbon, Alex Davis, Jason Arnopp, Kelley Armstrong, Catriona Ward, Mike Carey, John Connolly, Barbie Wilde, Pete & Nicky Crowther, Simon Clark and many, many more. Lastly, a big heartfelt thank you to my terrific family and especially my perfect wife Marie, who keeps me sane whenever all around me seems crazy. Love you more than anything.

Contents

Introduction

Dire implication in the title.

Whether anarchies entrapped…or desires suppressed. Enter or exit anywhere in this superb, conspiring collection; all armed or washed-out roads lead to Paul Kane's eloquent warnings. Fate, as usual, has big plans.

Kane's tales, in *The Controllers*, are ominous venoms; each a part of the book's larger mosaic of havoc and sabotage. As these tributaries merge, they suggest that, despite all karmas and loss, despite every sin and charity, every bleak cruelty or radiant triumph, we are nothing more, nor less, than casualties and Generals in wars of the heart. Resurrected, not by mystic odds, but by payment of our truest debts.

The stories unnerve and Kane's stellar writing is rich with high-tides of insight. Amid injustices and glory are no gravities that fail, no exits promised. To enter the book, is to be exquisitely trapped; it is a finely-tuned text of dread.

The Controllers.

Whether surveillances, or supervisions, Kane's stories are tours of damned prayers, found kingdoms. His imprisoned characters struggle to understand the forces at work, which torment and manipulate them and, for all those trapped in gulags of unknown circumstance, perhaps slipped between fractals, Kane neither supplies nor refuses redemption. In these fearing tales of captivity, are excruciating maps of each life; culpable or otherwise. In glorious passage-after-passage, annealed by regret or hope, Paul Kane suggests there is no prison, even ourselves, that is inescapable. That truth is belief and that destiny, however much we are prey to its seizure, must be reclaimed.

Richard Christian Matheson

Astral

I first discovered I had the astral talent at an early age, purely by accident. Initially I thought it to be a blessing, but I now know it is my curse. For I have seen things no human being should ever see. I have discovered our true place in the great scheme of things—our 'purpose'?—and this knowledge has plagued my waking existence ever since...

It started as I was approaching my fifteenth birthday, two years after my beloved twin sister Abigail departed from this world, the subject of a tragic riding accident. It was my misfortune to be struck down with a fever and I spent a week in bed, the sweat pouring out of my flesh so that the sheets around me remained perpetually soaked.

During this time I dreamt I was pulled up and out of my body. I spent many an hour simply watching myself restlessly thrashing around on the bed below. I know I probably should have been frightened by the experience, but I wasn't in the slightest bit alarmed. In fact I began to enjoy it—welcoming the opportunity to view myself as others saw me; as my mother looked upon me, sat by my bedside, a cloth in her hand to wipe my brow. She was especially worried now that I was her only remaining child.

When the fever lifted, I assumed the dreams had been caused by my illness and said nothing to my family. After all, many bizarre and wild visions had passed before my eyes during those seven days: things that couldn't possibly be real. Or so I judged to be accurate at that naive age.

It wasn't until later that I learned it hadn't been a dream at all. Not in the same way most people perceive the notion, at any rate.

Bored one night when sleep refused to visit me, I thought how wonderful it would be to float outside of myself as I had done when the fever gripped me. I missed the feeling of freedom it brought; the reassurance that I was no longer held back by the matter which encased me. Fuelled by an insatiable curiosity, I closed my eyes and willed myself upwards. To my astonishment it started to happen again. I felt the separation—it is not painful at all, but there is a mild sense of loss—as my ethereal form drifted towards the ceiling.

Though it was dark, I could see myself quite clearly in the bed. I looked asleep, peaceful and resting quietly. A thin length of light ran from my head to my floating self, rather like the safety rope a climber might wear. I was comforted by the fact that I would be able to find my way back at any time without worry. For a while I watched myself breathing in and out. I took in only minimal amounts of air, as if I were on the very brink of death itself. Yet somehow I felt no harm would come to me.

I began to wonder... could I move outside of the room? I had no cumbersome physical ties, so surely it was possible. All I had to do was will myself on.

I tried to clutch at the door handle. Instead of grasping the metal, my hand went straight through the door itself. Cautiously, I followed suit, and soon I was moving through our house.

On the landing I caught sight of myself in the mirror. I was a transparent shape tinged with delicate whiteness, wholly invisible to anyone outside of this plane.

I glided over my parents, asleep in the next room, then paid a visit to my grandfather who was staying with us for the holidays. But in addition to their bodies, I could also determine a glowing outline which surrounded them: their own auras, albeit steadfastly earthbound. Sadly, I could only travel for so long before the cord behind pulled me back into my own vessel.

As time went on and I became stronger, I began to experiment more and more with my power. No longer was I restricted to the house; I could roam around unhindered across countryside, past buildings, villages and towns. I saw as much of life as I dared, and never once did I have to leave my modest bedroom.

Anyone who noticed me lying on the bed or sitting in a chair would conclude that I was taking a nap, particularly if I decided to step out during the day, when in actual fact I was at the bottom of the ocean, or halfway up a mountainside. I examined every beautiful aspect of this world, but I would always be wrenched back when I'd strayed too far or been gone for too long.

It was my fantastic secret and I never revealed it to anyone. I feared not just the taunts of people who didn't believe, but also the attentions of those who did—who might seek to use me for their own ends (I needn't have worried). No, I travelled alone and kept the knowledge to myself. It was not in my nature to spy. In all the years I have been doing this, not once have I intruded upon another person's privacy. Not on purpose, that is.

By my mid-thirties I had been around the world several times, as well as journeying to its very core. It was incredible to be able to pass through solid substances like cheese-wire through clay.

And I had moved out into space. It had been years since I mastered the act of flying, soaring along with the birds in the open expanses of blue and white. It was joyous beyond compare. However, nothing could have prepared me for the splendours that lay out *there*. I swept through the heavens, a jet-black drape with pinpricks letting through light from behind.

I was no scientist, but I found it all fascinating. I loved to amble by those twinkling flecks and gaze at them. Oh the remarkable grace of it all! I was truly at home amongst the stars and felt like a god in the realm of the gods.

How little I knew.

But I refused to leave it at that, more's the pity. I began to push the envelope, to go where reality mixed with fantasy. In my ignorance I stumbled through into other dimensions. Colours spun into infinity and the whole universe turned itself inside out. Space became black stars upon a white background, and all that I knew to be absolute mingled bizarrely with insanity like paint on a canvas.

That's when I began to sense them.

As I pushed further on, something beckoned to me. Subconsciously or not, I couldn't tell, but I was definitely aware of a calling. I ordered my mind to follow the summons, though it would take me many attempts to finally locate the source.

I found myself falling into an odd mist which carried me along. It felt like I was being dragged sideways through a barrier. Reality no longer existed for me anymore as the strands of living smog swirled around my astral form. But still I followed the call, regardless of its destination. I experienced an uncontrollable need to do so.

When I finally broke through the veil, I came upon a place unlike any other in my experience: a nebulous world filled with sinister cities, encircled by volcano-like peaks which spat fire periodically; a white fire which I knew held no heat. The twisted, intricate streets of the cities, which curved and coiled back upon themselves like snakes, were lined with monoliths—all connected by interweaving conduits and bridges. I was high above them, observing from afar the figures that populated this locale: black dots walking quickly towards their destinations.

I did not feel the cold—how could I when my body was elsewhere?—but I shivered nonetheless. What was this strange vista? Where had my travels taken me this time? I wondered.

Ignoring my trepidation, I plunged myself towards the nearest megalopolis, always following the summons. The closer I came to the towers, those glistening obelisks, the more I could tell they were not made from any kind of stable substance. The surface of the buildings pulsed, and I saw thick tubular veins running up the side. I couldn't be sure, but it looked as if the structures were organic. Alive in some way. Indeed, I could have sworn the whole city was looking at me, right through me.

Wandering along those streets, I found my unease intensifying. The figures, so small from above, were now right in front of me... all around me. They were hooded beings who kept to the shade, shrouded in secrecy. But their cloaks seemed to cling to them, hugging each one like a second skin.

I watched them striding along their weird and distorted lanes: some in pairs, others in trios. They followed their hidden agendas, flitting from edifice to edifice, heads bowed, chanting insane mantras alien to my ears—yet somehow never out loud.

I decided to trail a pair inside one of the towers, staying a comfortable distance behind. Imagine my confusion at witnessing such sights, as the creatures made their way to hollowed-out alcoves, each with space for two or three of their kind. When they bent to sit down, seats sprang up that resembled obscene

fungi. It actually grew up out of the floor to accommodate them. I now firmly believe the material was responding to some form of mental command.

Opaque globes the size of goldfish bowls detached themselves from moist walls and came to float about the Hooded Ones like pets in search of attention. I could see pictures on the spheres, blurred at first, then clearer and clearer. Each image was of a different part of our—my—world; places I had been, sometimes even people I had 'met'. They were observing my home, just as I was observing theirs. Undetected, covertly, and with that same insatiable curiosity. But for what purpose?

Then I noticed that the figures' hoods were glimmering with a strange azure colour, and every time one of them reached out a pale, withered hand, something changed on those 'screens': a man stopped and went up a street he never set out to explore, only to encounter a robber wielding a knife; a small child slipped away from her parents and became lost in a crowd; a pianist injured his hands and lost the ability to play; a doctor prescribed the wrong dosage of medication to a patient with catastrophic results; a woman suddenly fell in love with someone she'd only just met, someone she didn't really know at all; an adventurer decided to tackle just one more expedition... his last; a husband chose that precise moment to smother his wife with a pillow; a military dictator reasoned that the time had come to expand his empire, at the cost of countless lives...

A plethora of minute details, interference in people's routines that amounted to total domination. Decisions 'controlled' one way or another by this mysterious race. Where we might think fate is to blame for the atrocious luck we're experiencing, that is not actually the case at all!

But their meddling did not stop there. Nature yielded to their authority as well, it appeared; for I beheld avalanches, earthquakes, hurricanes, blizzards, every manner of disaster one can think of, utilised in order to carry out their dreadful schemes.

I realised then that there must be billions of such globes in each tower, and that these Controllers (for want of a better name) were actually in charge of our destinies. A terrible feeling of helplessness

overwhelmed me at that moment. If these unspeakable creations had a hand in every part of our existence, were manipulating and guiding each human resolution, what was their goal in doing so? How long had we been but puppets to them? Was all the beauty of the world, the stars, the heavens, simply a framework for some Machiavellian conspiracy? Were we but cattle in the field, herded onwards? And if so, where were we being led? *My Lord, who were these people?*

The call came again, disturbing me. It was much more anxious this time and I could do nothing but leave the Controllers to 'their' affairs.

It drew me downwards to the very centre of their world, where I came to a great ellipse of what appeared to be water; cool, blue liquid in a gigantic lake. The sounds were coming from that location and I swooped down to hover by the side of the crevice where it rested. At this distance I could see that although the texture of the lake was rippling, it was not like any kind of water I'd ever come across. There was a film over the top which bulged and gently vibrated, and I recognised more of the worm-like veins around its massive edge; set in the slimy ground so that it resembled a rare mineral floating in tar.

Suddenly the surface shifted and I could see objects floating around beneath. I took them to be monstrous entities at first glance, but as they rose up I saw instead that they were people. Faces, bodies; all human, but altered. There was nothing tangible about them. They were merely outlines... or reflections? Had this collection of haunted wraiths reached out to me, trapped in the blueness with no possibility of release?

And there, almost submerged by the others, was the physiognomy of my dearest sister Abigail. Though it was hard to be sure, I thought she mouthed the words "Help me!" before being pushed aside by more of the orb's residents.

I was about to head inside after her when a thin slip of grimy tissue snapped over the ellipse. Within seconds it had moved back again, and there was no sign of the multitude beneath.

I knew then that it was a living optic of sorts, which had just blinked—incredible as that may seem. And it was this animated

oracle that had sought my attention, for reasons beyond my understanding. The source of power for the city—for their world—flashed white, and visions entered my mind. I was being shown things, extraordinary things I could never have imagined. About the Controllers. Past, present and future, the Eye transferred its information to me at tremendous speed. I do not think it could prevent itself.

But the flow was interrupted by several of the Hooded Ones appearing at the Eye's rim. This time they could see me as I saw them. They knew I was there all right; had probably known all along. More joined them, and more, and still more; until there was a legion of Controllers around the ridge.

In unison they stripped off their hoods, and I just gained a quick glimpse of their appearance before a terrific agony set in. The cowls, as I'd surmised, were indeed a part of them. They peeled these back like scabs on spots to reveal repugnantly thin, piebald flesh, marked with protruding bones. They were hairless and possessed no features other than singular cyan eyes in the middle of their heads, just like the larger one they were all gathered around.

It was the light from their lenses, a combined effort, which I found too much to bear. I still don't know to this day how I could feel the shafts of burning torment they drove into me, but I assure you it was quite real at the time, and intense enough to make me lose consciousness after only a brief exposure.

The next thing I knew, I was awake on my bed. I can only imagine that my body pulled me back along its safety cord at that precise moment, and thus I escaped the fate those bastards had in mind for me.

Or perhaps they let me go intentionally, knowing I could never tell the population my tale without risking confinement to an institution. I cannot even bring myself to inform you of their horrific plans. Do not worry, though, you'll find out for yourself soon enough.

And try as I might, I cannot find my way back to their reality, or to Abigail. In my, now infrequent, journeys I am restricted to our own spectrum, as once I was to my parents' house. Only in

my sleep, in my nightmares, do I go there time and time again.

Yet I feel certain I will be called back again at some point: probably on the day I rise up from my body a final time and cannot return to it. Perhaps I shall become part of the Eye with my sister, feeding it in some unconscionable way, entangled in the blue?

My greatest wish is that before I take my place there, I am allowed a few fleeting moments to look upon my world, no matter how tainted I know it to be. To take pleasure in my travels and dance between the stars without a care, as I did before I discovered the truth.

Perhaps then I might even take that astral peace with me, to draw upon when all else seems hopeless...

Eye of the *Beholder*

The *Beholder* is ageless.

Since time immemorial it has subsisted at the kernel of its world. At the centre. *The junction.* Enormous and blue, a great eye with veins snaking away from its side, outstretching into the vastness beyond.

And it sees everything. Absolutely everything.

Occasionally it feels the souls trapped beneath its thin, diaphanous outer-layer, struggling to escape. (Like floaters in any conventional eyeball.) They push up towards the surface, sensing that if they could only break through this barrier they would be free. But each time they come too near, the *Beholder* blinks, pulling its dark eyelid over the top and dispersing them, clearing its vision. Their anguish empowers it, juices the realm above and enables the fundamental work to continue.

Now, as was its wont, the *Beholder* allows itself to rise mentally through the blanket of dirt that keeps it hidden. That keeps it safe. It gazes upon the many cities which make up its world, surrounded by a strange mist that sequesters this place from the rest of reality. It watches the autochthonous volcanoes spew forth their cold, anaemic fire, and observes the figures flitting about in the dark streets below. Secret, hooded beings that band together in twos and threes. Its children and its protectors. Hurrying, they make their way along the Byzantine patchwork of passages and gennels, along winding roads and down twisting alleyways; their incantations spoken without words. The *Beholder* goes with them all, following each one individually to its destination—in the spear-shaped living towers they call home.

Each hooded entity has its own special post in the minarets, its own niche. Hollowed-out bowers they can claim as their own: where the organic framework of the steeple's interior will respond to their singular wishes and requirements. Seats instinctively bulge up for them to sit at, growing out of the floor, and the perfectly clear globes they use to view and 'control' customarily leap out from the walls to gather about them, each one displaying images from another place, another world. A blue-white planet they have no name for, but which its natives insist upon calling Earth.

It intrigued the *Beholder* to see where they came from, the spirits bound inside its own bulk. Where they began and where they ended. One of its brood bent forwards, an almost turquoise glow shimmering from beneath its unusual cowl. The *Beholder* knew that under the hood—itself a functioning part of its entirety: a protective second skin—its face was a map of bones, held in check by a tight, mottled, and hairless covering of flesh. And in the middle was a single cerulean eye not unlike its own. Indeed, it was the *Beholder*'s gift to them. A miniature representation of itself they carried with them. The key to their abilities.

And their inheritance.

The *Beholder* watched as its ancillary watched. A life just beginning on the 'screen'. White liquid gushing out, containing hundreds of millions of microscopic life-forms. It observed as they swam upstream, fighting against the tide. Many died along the way but some, the strongest, made it to the finish line. Yet there could be only one winner in this race. One survivor. The choice was made—it had been made even before they were discharged. The victor butted its way inside, leaving its companions to perish on the outskirts. The egg, so smooth and round like the *Beholder*'s eye, was fertilised. Ready to be nurtured to size. Would it be twins or perhaps malformed? No, not this time. The embryo developed normally, by fourteen weeks limbs and internal organs in place, and now all that remained was growth. Any one of a billion things could have gone wrong during the course of the pregnancy both outside and in. But they didn't. It was routine in every way, apart from the mother experiencing a touch of heartburn now and again (only a sign that it had a full head of hair according to old wives' tales); that and the requisite aching back. The small human hibernated, comfortable and warm in amniotic fluid, for a little over nine months. The most peaceful and content it would ever feel in its entire life.

There followed an easy birth as well. No Herculean labour or caesarean section. Let it come naturally; the time for sorrow would soon find it... her (as now the *Beholder* came to think of it as a girl—a baby girl called Lucy). The *Beholder* scrutinised, but never interfered. That was not its intent, nor its purpose. It left such things to the creatures inhabiting this domain.

Maybe cot-death might claim her, is that what its progeny had in mind? No, it would let her live... for now. The first real scare would be the illness that came like an amateur assassin in the night, serious enough to warrant several days back in hospital. Thank God her parents had found her in time, barely breathing. No, not God. The *Beholder* knew whom they should really be thanking. For not only was the hooded one directing the life of this child—its long, pallid fingers stabbing the air, provoking incidents—but that of her parents as well, adding more worry to their day-to-day existences, encouraging them not to have any more children.

But how glad they'd been when their Lucy was released, able now to celebrate her second birthday—while all the time, at the back of their minds, they wondered whether something else would happen. Whether she'd be taken from them someday.

Not yet. There was still much to do.

The daughter grew, filling out her new body, muscles strengthening, bones developing with each intake of calcium, hair turning from blonde to brown and spreading down past her shoulders.

The world was a fantastic place, Lucy learnt. Beautiful, colourful and bright. But it could also be a place of anger and insecurity. Of agony and tears. Too many close calls to recount: the time she put her hand out to stroke a relative's puppy and it bit her, sharp needle-teeth puncturing her skin, acquainting her with blood for the first time; falling off the swing in her back garden and grazing her knee on the hard ground; a drink of water going down the wrong way and taking her breath for a moment; the sensation of touching a fireguard and burning her fingers—no, Lucy hadn't liked that at all. And the memory of being shouted at for opening the gates and nearly making it to the roadside (oh, but the cars were so, so pretty…), her daddy's face turning so red she thought it might just explode.

School presented Lucy with a whole new set of problems, for although she was fairly quick to learn, one of the older teachers took an immediate and vehement dislike to her. She would later learn it was because of some trick her dad had played on the tutor when *he* had attended the school. Lucy found herself being punished for things she hadn't done. It was always her talking in class, even though she was paying complete attention to the teacher's oration. Basically it was a mess. No one was happy, not the teacher, not the pupil and certainly not her parents, who demanded to know why their little girl came home crying four out of five nights a week.

Finally it all came out one evening and, after a blazing row down at the school, during which the headmaster had defended the member of staff in question to the hilt, their daughter was moved to another educational facility. Already behind with her studies because of the upset at home and at school, Lucy was forced to play catch-up, which, to her credit, she did quite admirably. However, this reputation as a troublemaker stuck with her, and she was never really given the opportunity to show what she could do—left out of sports teams and school plays purposely (she felt). It followed her right up to secondary school, where she also found herself the target for bullies because of her miserable disposition—unaware as they were that ever since her menstrual cycle had started to turn, she'd suffered from terrible bouts of depression.

On one occasion they'd waited for Lucy to begin the walk to the bus-stop after school and dragged her behind a hedge. Careful not to leave any incriminating marks, they pinned her to the floor and forced her to eat dirt and grass, then stole her bag with her books, homework and purse inside. She'd learnt her lesson about telling tales, though, and simply said she'd mislaid it—for which she was grounded until the end of term.

Lucy did make some friends, thankfully, and to those who openly sought her companionship she gave loyalty without question in return. But then along came boys and she was soon forgotten about as her pals—once the most ardent of men-haters—chose to spend all their time with members of the opposite sex. Given half a chance Lucy might well have joined them, but her self-esteem had never been up to much and those pictures in magazines or on TV didn't help either, celebrating the statuesque figure of the supermodel or the voluptuous curves of the page-three girl. What she saw when she looked in the mirror was a Plain Jane with braces on her teeth and spots on her face.

So Lucy decided to devote herself to her studies instead, gearing herself up for the big exams she'd take at the end of the school year. Exams that would be her key to bigger and better things. She loved writing and pictured herself one day working in a newspaper office—if her grades were good enough, that was.

Regrettably her parents chose that particular time to break up; well, you could hardly blame them after Dad found out Mum had been seeing a younger man while he was at work: an electrician who lived across the road from them, the subject of many a young girl's fantasies… including Lucy's. Her mum left with this hunk to go and live ten miles away in a small rented flat, the aftermath of a particularly nasty row in which Lucy's father had even raised his fists, though never followed through.

Her emotions all over the place, Lucy screwed up just about every single exam. Words like 'extenuating' and 'circumstances' were bandied about, but the long and the short of it was she'd have to resit if she wanted to get anywhere. Disillusioned by the whole thing, she opted to leave school with just a D in Physics and Maths, and an E in English, drawing dole while she got her 'head together'. Comfort eating became her biggest weakness, sat watching soaps and talk shows on daytime TV… possibly where the notion came from in the first place. Then again, maybe not. Later she'd bring it all up in the bathroom, just in time to welcome her dad home from a hard day's work at the car plant.

He encouraged her to get out more, pass more time with people her own age. So she did. Her weekends, and eventually weeknights too, were spent in town, where she discovered a whole other scene and got entangled with some very suspect characters. But for once in her life she felt like she belonged. Lucy got invited to some extremely private parties and indulged herself freely, the comfort eating quickly replaced by more hazardous pursuits. It was at one such soirée that she met her first boyfriend. He called himself Ziggy (it wasn't his real name, he just used it because he thought he looked like a famous singer—or was it because he didn't want anyone knowing his true identity?) and Lucy really thought he was 'the one'.

"You're gorgeous, you know," he used to tell her, before sticking his hand up her jumper and fumbling around with her on a bed that wasn't even theirs. And it was more or less true; Lucy was very attractive now that the braces and acne had gone. But it wasn't long before she found out Ziggy was sleeping around with most of the women she considered friends, feeding them all the same lines before pouncing. To get back at him, Lucy did the same: parading a string of faceless males in front of him and bedding them all with a mixture of delight and remorse.

The warped dream of her late teens came to a shocking conclusion, though, when one of the guests at a party choked on his own vomit after foolishly mixing spirits and hard-core drugs. An ambulance was called and the police weren't far behind, detaining some and arresting others—including Ziggy (real name Vincent Day) who it turned out was a pretty proficient dealer in his spare time. The jolt of being questioned by the police, not to mention seeing that guy's fresh cadaver on the floor of the bathroom—spittle and dried sick forming a halo around his head—was enough to snap her out of her reverie.

Lucy's dad, summoned to pick her up from the station (no charges this time, only a caution), wasn't as angry as she thought he'd be. He just seemed tired, and so *old* that day.

He helped her get over the addictions she'd picked up the best way he knew how, with love and succour. Eventually she got her life back on track, securing herself a job at a pet shop, in spite of her long-standing fear of dogs, and saving up her money as opposed to blowing it all on cheap thrills. She made new friends, *better* friends, and started to enjoy herself more and more. In her early twenties she'd experience some of the best times she was ever likely to know. This included meeting Greg, the pet shop owner's son, who arrived home from his three-year university course in Business and Media Management one day, bumping into her—literally—as he entered the shop.

"I'm so sorry," he said, helping her pick up the bags of bird nuts she'd been carrying. And that was that. The next thing she knew they were dating. Real dates, not the wham-bams she was used to. This was love, no doubt about it, and it definitely put her fling with Ziggy into perspective.

Then came another crisis. There was this disease, she'd read about it in all the papers, seen it on the news. And it wasn't just confined to the gay community as the experts had first thought. No, this plague had spread outwards and apparently you could catch it from sharing needles or from having sex without protection. Not only that, this disease could kill you—stone-dead. Lucy thought about the many men at those parties, the drugs available. Weeks, months of agonising, of keeping Greg at arm's length. Should she tell him of her past and risk losing everything they had together? Would he understand if she went to be tested? Would he ever be able to trust her again?

It was so humiliating, confessing all, but her fears had proved groundless. Their relationship, and Greg, was much stronger than that. He even went with her and took a test himself. But then there was more waiting, more doubts, more self-recrimination, before they finally discovered they were both clean.

They'd only been sleeping together a few months when she skipped a period. For the first time Lucy missed the all-encompassing gloom that arrived and settled in for one week out of every four. No, she *urged* it to come, because at least then she'd know she wasn't... But how could she be? They'd taken precautions, after what she'd been through she'd insisted. The injustice of it, after all those years of... for it to happen now that she'd found someone... someone truly special.

More sleepless nights. Building up to telling Greg again. She'd wanted to do it the day she found out, but he'd been so full of his own good news: a brand new job working on promotions for a multiplex cinema chain with, more importantly, decent rates of pay. She didn't have the heart to bring him down.

Nevertheless the time came when she *had* to say something, before it was too late—regardless of the fact she'd already decided to keep the baby. Much to her surprise, and great relief, Greg was delighted and asked her if she wanted to get a place with him. She hated leaving her dad after everything he'd done, but he was over the moon for the pair of them. Her mum, likewise, now living on her own after the fling with the electrician had blown a fuse. So they set up home together, Greg and Lucy, and she revelled in every sublime minute of it. Choosing furniture for their small—cosy—bungalow; arranging colour schemes; getting everything just right. It more than made up for the morning sickness. Greg's father gave her plenty of time off from the shop, after all it was *his* grandchild she was carrying.

They settled in nicely, and although it was never spoken out loud, both of them knew that the ensuing stage in their relationship would probably be marriage... perhaps once the baby was born.

The accident came right out of the blue. Greg was on his way to London to find sponsors for an independent film festival, when the train he was on derailed. It wasn't the worst catastrophe the rail service had suffered in its time, in fact they were lucky more people hadn't been killed—or so the TV newsman had announced that night. Seventeen injured, mostly just minor cuts and bruises.

Three dead.

Lucy remembered Greg kissing her on the forehead that morning before leaving, then placing a hand on her stomach.

"Take care of Kicker," he'd said, grinning as he used the baby's nickname.

"I will," she promised.

They were the last words ever to pass between them.

The severe burden of grief, the sheer weight of loss, was tremendous. The father of her child had been alive one minute, was dead the next. Where was the fairness in that? What was the purpose? Out on the streets were rapists, muggers, killers... roaming free, healthy and... and the nicest man ever to walk... He was...

The months following the funeral were devastating. Lucy couldn't afford to keep up payments on the bungalow, and so she moved out. Wasn't as if she wanted to stay there now anyway. It had been *their* place, meant for a couple. A family.

She went back to live with her dad, but swallowed her pride and finally accepted financial help from Greg's parents. Lucy's mum came back to see her, to be with her child in her hour of need; it was written all over her face that she wanted to make amends. She ended up staying permanently, getting back together with her estranged husband after all these years. They guided Lucy through the last stages of her pregnancy, and were there at the hospital as she endured a staggering nineteen-hour labour—the doctors almost lost Lucy twice—the product of which was Anne, a healthy seven-pound baby girl.

After that, her daughter took priority. Lucy was too busy to think about her heartache, except on off-days or in the quiet moments just before dawn. *Life goes on*, she'd tell herself. Indeed it did, for her, for little Annie, and for her parents, who now seemed more in love than they'd ever been before.

She went through the highs and lows of bringing up a baby as a single parent, and with friends and family around her Lucy just about coped. She hadn't been looking for more complications in her life, but just as before fate (if she only knew) pushed her in a certain direction and she met Richard in the supermarket one day. At first she wasn't sure, not this soon after Greg. But she couldn't help how she felt about him, and it was blatantly obvious he felt the same way.

Lucy worried about introducing him to Anne, now five going on forty-five. But the pair hit it off straight away. Her parents applauded Lucy's choice, a handsome banker with a house and a charming disposition. Okay, so he was divorced, but then everyone has baggage. Even Greg's family gave her their blessing, once she'd assured them they would never have cause to feel left out.

This time Lucy did marry, and she had another baby. A son, who she felt compelled to call Gregory. Not many men would have been okay with that, but Richard was. Once again Lucy experienced a period of joy. Not total joy—for can such a thing ever exist?—but close enough to be mistaken for the real thing without closer inspection. Lucy was even looking into home study courses, finally resitting her exams before attempting a degree the same way. Maybe she hadn't left it too late after all, and that job as a journalist was out there somewhere just waiting for her.

Then came the night of the fire.

Richard was out of town for the weekend on business, Anne was at her grandparents, on Greg's side, while Lucy and little Gregory were back at the homestead enjoying a quality mother-son break together.

Some time between two and three o'clock on Sunday morning—or so the investigators said—there was an unexplained electrical surge in the kitchen that caused the fridge's plug to catch light, sparks from which ignited the writing pad on the kitchen top, bearing a list of groceries for that week's shopping trip. The fire then fanned out, fuelled by the wood-effect cupboards and the kitchen blinds. Within minutes the tiles on the kitchen floor were starting to melt and the hallway carpet was ablaze. This set off the smoke-alarm but the battery was flat and it only managed a few exhausted beeps before expiring. Lucy began to cough as the tendrils of smog rose and entered her room, seeping under the door. It took her a while to wake up, but once she did she instinctively understood what was happening and called the emergency services using the cordless phone, recharging on the bedside table.

Then, staggering onto the landing, she found herself engulfed in a thick, black cloud. Lucy fought to reach Gregory's room and gathered up the barely conscious toddler in her arms. She made for the window, but realised that the drop into the garden was too big a gamble to take. If she'd still been in the bungalow it wouldn't have been a problem. Their only option was to go downstairs and get out through the front door.

Barking like a dog as the smoke took its toll, Lucy wrapped her boy in a blanket and ran back out onto the landing. She aimed for the staircase, its vague outline barely discernible in the dense, deadly fog. The floor creaked and the heat from below scolded her bare feet through the boards—her slippers left neglected by the bed in her room. Lucy reached the first step and, using the wall as a guide, began to descend. A tongue of fire lapped at them from the hall, through the banister rail. Lucy kept her head down, holding her son as close as she possibly could. She was almost at the bottom when the staircase gave way, pitching them into the hall.

Lucy screamed as the fire bit into her, but she rolled over onto her front; the fear of crushing Gregory outweighed by the terrible danger the fire posed to him. It fused her nightdress to her back, set her hair alight and robbed her arms of skin. Her feet and legs bubbled with the intensity of the flames, making it impossible to even crawl. The pain was unlike anything she'd ever imagined, let alone experienced, but it soon reached a crescendo and Lucy's whole body seemed to go numb.

She lay there for an eternity.

Then Lucy thought she heard noises, a banging perhaps: it was hard to tell above the roaring of the fire. She tried to look through dried up eyes. The front door! There *was* hope after all.

But it was only the illusion of hope. Lucy's consciousness was ebbing away, even as the axe forced its way through the wood. Even as the men wearing breathing apparatus broke in and located her, dragging her out to the premature applause of the crowd now watching on the street. She woke up just once after that, as they were loading her into the ambulance. Lucy wanted to speak, to ask about little Gregory, but her voice eluded her. So instead she looked up at the paramedic, trying to communicate her question telepathically. The woman was too busy attempting to stabilise her to notice.

"Looks like full thickness. Seventy, maybe eighty percent," Lucy heard her say. Nothing about her son, though.

"How's the kid?" somebody else asked.

"He's alive."

As soon as she heard this, Lucy slipped silently away. She would never know what happened after her passing: the fact that little Gregory would have breathing difficulties throughout his youth and into early adulthood because of that night; that Richard was called back from his business trip (from his mistress' bed if the truth be known) to identify his wife's horrifically scorched body, and then lived the rest of his pitiful life plagued with guilt about where he'd been when the fire broke out; that Anne would wish she'd been there that night, too, thinking perhaps she could have done *something*—little realising that by sending her away her mother had fulfilled a promise made before Annie was even born; that this trauma would finally trigger the stroke that had been waiting to attack her dad for years; and that her mum would mourn forever the loss of her little baby girl.

A baby born just yesterday in the distorted recesses of her memory.

There Lucy's story ended. An average story, more tragic than some, less so than others—no child abuse, no poverty, no prison, no deformities. Three and a half decades of life, her existence making its mark, however modest. Her tale intertwined with, rebounding off, and affecting so many more. But it was still only a blink of an eye for the *Beholder*.

It drew her now into its bowels, to join the infinite number of souls confined there. Briefly it wondered what she would think when she learned the truth; the reason why she'd been born, why she'd died. It wondered how she'd react when she realised the whole of her existence had been controlled by the hooded one with the globe. Every action, every event, every decision. That at the quiver of a mouldering finger she might never have existed at all. Or, conversely, lived to a ripe old age in a retirement home— incapable even of going to the toilet on her own. In the end it didn't really matter. She'd served her purpose adequately. That was the important thing.

The *Beholder* knew that its own child would now turn its attention to another beginning, another seed and egg. Another Lucy. (No, there would never be another Lucy. It had the decency to recognise that much at least.)

As for itself, well the great eye would watch and wait. But never interfere. Because that was not its intent. Nor its purpose.

It left such things to the creatures inhabiting this domain.

The Pain Cages

Ask someone to describe pain.

They might say, the feeling they get when they stub their toe on a table, or accidentally hit their thumb with a hammer when they're banging a nail into the wall. Pain can be more than merely physical, of course. It can hurt when a marriage breaks up or a loved one dies. That's even harder to put into words.

But these are all just shadows, echoes of something much greater.

Pain, *true* pain, is impossible to describe—no matter how hard anyone tries. It can rip apart a person's soul, leaving them a shell of what they once were. And if it is hard to endure, it is certainly much harder to watch.

For some.

This story is about pain, in all its forms. We enter this world screaming and crying as we fight to take our first breath, being struck on the back to rouse us into consciousness. Most of us leave this world the same way: with a jolt. If we're lucky it will be quick, if we're not...

This story is about pain.

True pain.

One

The piercing screams wake me.

Not straight away, but slowly. They sound as if they're coming from a million miles away. The closer to consciousness I draw, though, the louder they are, like someone turned up the volume on a stereo: surround sound, sub woofers, the works. Then I realise they're not part of some strange dream, but coming from the real world.

From somewhere nearby.

I open my eyes, or at least I try to. I never would have thought it could be so difficult; the amount of times I've taken this simple action for granted. But now… Actually I can't tell whether they're open or shut because it's still so dark and I can't really feel my eyelids. My guts are doing somersaults; I feel like I need to be sick.

And all the while the screaming continues.

My face—my whole body—is pressed up against a hard, solid surface. I'm lying on a smooth but cold floor, curled up like a cat in front of a fireplace, though nowhere near as contented. I try to lift my head. I thought it was difficult to open my eyes, but this is something else entirely. Jesus, it hurts—a shockwave travelling right down the length of my neck and spine. Instinctively my hand goes out to clutch at my back, but I can't move that either. *Must have been one hell of a bender last night.* And the screaming? Had to be a TV somewhere, someone watching a really loud horror film with no thought for anyone else. Wait, had I turned it on after managing to get back home in God alone knows what state?

This is the weirdest hangover ever. I have some of the symptoms—head feels like it's caving in, aching all over, stomach churning… But my tongue doesn't feel like someone's been rubbing it with sandpaper. I'm not thirsty from dehydration. Maybe someone slipped something into my glass?

Maybe you took something voluntarily. Wouldn't be the first time.

There's movement to my left and my head whips sideways. I immediately regret it as stars dance across my field of vision. I still can't see anything, even after the universe of stars fade. Now I realise some sick son of a bitch has put a blindfold over my eyes.

More movement, this time to the right. I try to lift my hands to pull down the material, but again they won't budge. My fingertips brush against metal and now I know why I can't move them. It's not because of any fucking hangover: I'm handcuffed. My fingers explore further and find a chain attached to the cuffs…

The manacles?

When I hear the screams again, the terror racked up a notch, it dawns on me that I'm in a whole world of trouble. Maybe my groggy condition made me slow on the uptake, I don't know, or perhaps I just couldn't acknowledge the shouts of agony as real. But they are; there's no doubting that now. And I'm definitely suffering from the after-effects of drugs, just not in the way I thought. Drugs designed to knock me out rather than get me high.

More movement, this time a swishing sound in front and behind me at the same time. How is that possible? My heart's pumping fast, breath coming in heavy gasps. I try to say something but all that comes out are a series of odd grunts.

"Sshh," whispers a voice. Can't tell whether it's a man or a woman, but they're close. "Keep quiet, and stay still!"

The advice seems sound, but I've never been one for taking any kind of orders. I pull at the chains holding my hands in front of me. Now I realise my feet are shackled too.

"Do as he says," comes another hushed voice, this one definitely a woman, "or you're going to get yourself killed."

"And us with him," spits the first person.

Killed? What the fuck? So many questions. Where am I? Who are these people talking to me? Why can I feel heat on my face? Smell something burning? No… cooking. Like roasting meat on a barbeque.

Struggling again, I scrape my face against the floor, trying to pull down the blindfold. The screams reach a fever pitch, mixed with pleas for help. The cloying smell is in my nose, down my throat; I gag.

I nose at the ground like a horse eating hay… and the blindfold slips a fraction. I can see a little through my right eye. There isn't a lot of light, but I see metal bars in front of me, all around me. A glimpse of the cages on either side: a man, no more than forty, cowering in the corner of his. A woman—the one who'd told me I'd get myself killed—is transfixed by something in front of her, tears tracking down her cheeks.

I follow her gaze and wish I hadn't.

I see the shape, the thing in yet another of these round cages. It's smoking, charred almost black, but here and there are patches of pink. A tuft or two of singed hair at the top of what must have been its head. Its eyeballs have melted, the liquid running down its cheeks, viscous and thick; flesh pulled taut over teeth that gleam so brightly they could have been used in a toothpaste commercial. This hunk of burnt flesh I'm looking at is—*was*—a person. That makes the stench even more pungent. Just that bit more sickening.

I notice the screaming has stopped. It must have been coming from inside that cage as the flames did their worst before petering out.

It feels like I'm watching the body for hours, but it can't be more than a minute.

Then, without any warning, the burnt figure lurches forward. No screams this time—its vocal chords are jelly—but its body rattles against the bars of the cage, which swings, suspended above the ground (as we all are).

Flesh, and what's left of the person's clothes, have stuck to the bottom of the cage, coming away from its body like molten plastic and revealing more raw pinkness. It makes only one last-ditch attempt for freedom before collapsing, never to move again.

This time I really do throw up, seeing stars again as the blindfold slips back over my eye. *Too late. I've seen it now. I can't ever forget...*

When I pass out I barely notice the transition—darkness replaced by darkness, black with black.

But I still see that body, hanging. A scorched mess that had once been human.

The ghosts of its screams following me back now into the void.

Interlude: Twenty Years Ago

This happened to me when I was ten; still holding on to childhood for grim death, in no particular hurry to be an adult.

I grew up on a council estate away from the city—farms and fields within walking distance. The houses were all uniform grey, there was a small park that the older kids wrecked periodically, and the council failed to keep any of the streets tidy. Old women gossiped over fences while young girls left school and became baby-making machines so they could live off benefits for the next twenty or thirty years.

Mum and Dad were still together back then. She worked part-time in a bookies and he worked on the busses. At family gatherings I'd sometimes hear my Uncle Jim telling people Mum could have done so much better than Dad. "With her looks, she could have had her pick!"

He was right about my mum, though. She was beautiful in a film star kind of way, all blonde hair and curls like Marilyn Monroe or Jean Harlow, and even at that age she'd lost none of the glamour. Sure, Dad was boring, but I like to think she ended up with him because he was a kind man with a kind face. In the end she did 'do better' as my Uncle would have called it, running off with owner of the bookies. She ended up with money, but was as miserable as sin. And, we suspected, the guy beat her. While my dad wallowed in a tiny flat, getting drunk until his liver just gave up the ghost. But that's another story, and long after this one.

I first saw The Monster one Bank Holiday. Dad was working overtime, but Mum had the day off. I was an only child, so had to amuse myself a lot of the time. That day I was getting under my mother's feet while she was trying to watch some musical on TV.

"Christopher Edward Warwick, do you have to make such a row!" she finally bawled. I couldn't really blame her: I'd turned the whole house into a spaceship and was busy piloting it into the deeper reaches of the Galaxy, battling one-eyed aliens with veiny skins.

She sent me out to play with the other kids, but that wasn't really my thing. I ended up wandering off to explore what the locals called 'The Cut'. I never understood why, because it didn't look like anyone had cut the grass down there in centuries. Maybe it was because a pitiful excuse for a canal ran the length of it like a wound. Here I could pretend that I was in the jungle where giant snakes and lions lived, and down by the water there were man-eating crocodiles (in actual fact you were more likely to find used condoms and fag ends).

I didn't come down here very often, not many kids did, but on that day I wandered further than I meant to—up a winding path to a small iron bridge crossing the canal. There I played Pooh sticks, something I hadn't done since I was six or seven—dropping twigs in the water on one side of the bridge to see which ones would come out first on the other. Not much of a game, but the snakes and lions appeared to be hiding today.

There were only a handful of twigs lying around, so when these were gone I went into the undergrowth to find more. I hadn't gone that far in when I found the den. It was covered up with foliage; quite well hidden beneath the trees, a hollowed out bit of green with earth for the floor and the remains of a fire. It was empty. I figured it must have been the older kids that had made it, looking for a private place to hang out.

At that age caution always ran a close second to curiosity, so I dropped the twigs and went inside. There was a strange smell, a toilet smell. I was about to leave when I spotted something towards the back, pages scattered.

A glimpse of something that, until today, had been forbidden.

I crept further in, certain that the older kids had been here because they'd left behind an Aladdin's Cave of porn. The magazines were screwed up, the pages creased—yet the pictures of half naked women posing for the camera were a revelation. At that age the girls in my class were just pests, there to torment, but this was different. These weren't girls, they were *women*, and they were showing me parts of their bodies willingly, opening up as easily as I was opening the pages.

I began to feel stirrings, a pleasant sensation as I ogled the photos. Then something fell out of one of the magazines. A piece of paper with handwritten scribblings all over it. I bent and picked it up, but could barely make out the spider scrawl. All except one phrase, written time and time again: 'They watch, and they wait.'

I frowned, then checked more of the magazines. I hadn't gotten very far when I heard the snapping of twigs I'd left in the entranceway. I spun and saw my monster. It was big, hairy, and its skin was almost black. It wore an old trenchcoat that strained tight at the shoulders. When it opened its mouth to speak I saw rotting teeth inside. Drool spilled onto its beard as it gargled, "Did *They* send you?"

I shook with terror. My erection shrank away and I dropped the magazine, a couple more of the handwritten sheets slipping out onto the floor. His wide, staring eyes followed them down. He covered the distance between us easily, grabbing hold of my arm—so hard I thought it might break. He towered above me. "They did, didn't They, boy." It wasn't a question. His fetid breath almost caused me to pass out.

I shook my head, unable to form any words.

"Yes. They've sent a little spy!"

"P-P-Please don't hurt me," I spluttered.

He yanked my arm. "I'm not going back!" he shouted. "You hear me? *Never.*"

I nodded. He seemed pleased that he'd got through to me. Then he drew me in so close I could see the insects living in his beard. "You go back, you tell Them that, boy," he growled.

He let me go. I gaped, but suddenly my natural survival instinct kicked in and I ran out of there. I plunged through the undergrowth, catching my forehead on the branch of a low-hanging tree. I fell; hard. Shaking my head, then casting a glance over my shoulder, I got up and began running again.

I felt the wetness at my temple, but didn't stop. I ran up that path, never looking back in case the 'monster' had decided to give chase.

I'm never going back… Never!

When I got home my mother said, "For God's sake, Chris, whatever have you been doing?" She took me into the kitchen, washed the cut on my head, then put some antiseptic on it. When she asked me again what I'd done, whether it had happened playing, all I could do was stare, opening and closing my mouth.

"Christopher Edward Warwick," she said a final time, "you tell me what happened, right now!"

"M-Monster… C-Canal," was all I could say.

"You and that blasted imagination of yours," she said. "Go to your room!"

When the truth emerged a day or so later, she felt pretty bad. I heard that some of the older boys had stumbled upon my monster and given him a good kicking before telling their parents, who called the police. He'd gone by the time they got there, but it was all around the estate about what had happened: that some pervo nutter had been living rough down by the bridge.

Mum hugged me when she when found out. She never said anything, but she knew. Knew the monster had been real.

I know better now—he wasn't really a monster at all. Just someone who knew the truth, and it had sent him insane.

'They watch and wait' he had written.

They watch and wait.

Two

When I wake up again, the blindfold is gone.

I open my eyes and look around. The bars are still there in front of me, I'm still shackled by the hands and feet, but the bonds are looser, my hands apart. I can move a little, manoeuvre myself up into a sitting position. I don't ache as much now, either. I wonder how much time has passed since—

Then I remember. The person burnt alive. It's gone now, the cage empty, the body taken away while I was unconscious.

"Welcome back," says the man who'd told me to be quiet, hanging in his own cage like a canary. He's wearing what look like sweatpants and a top, the kind of thing you'd find people dressed in at a country health spa.

"We thought you were out for the count," adds the woman who'd also spoken to me before. She's perhaps in her late twenties, with a slender frame—or what I can see of it beneath the smock she's wearing. Her dirty-blonde hair is matted with sweat; looks like it hasn't been washed in a couple of weeks. "How do you feel?"

"How… how do I *feel?*" I snap, a mixture of confusion and anger.

The man throws me a vicious look. "Christ, can't you keep it down? I told you before."

"I'll keep it down when somebody tells me what the fuck's going on," I yell at him, returning his glare with one of my own. I pull at the chains, testing their length.

"If you do that, they'll just make them tighter," the woman warns.

"Who will? And who did that…" Words fail me so I simply point across at the empty space where the charred body had once been.

"You ask far too many questions." This comes from another speaker, his voice richer, deeper. I turn and see yet another of the cages behind. In it an olive-skinned man sits crossed-legged, dressed like the first guy: in loose clothing. A prisoner's outfit.

"What's that supposed to mean? Who the fuck are you?"

"That's two more," he says.

I make to get up, about to grip the bars of the cage.

"I wouldn't, if I were you," the olive-skinned man tells me.

"Well you're not m—" Too late I see the wire curled around the bars, and no sooner have I touched the metal than I feel the electric shock. It ripples through my body, not strong enough to put me out again, but enough to blister my hands. "Shit!"

Is that what happened to the person in the cage in front? I wonder. *Did someone just leave the current on—running across the bottom as well—long enough to set fire to the poor sod inside?*

"I did warn you," says the man, his dark brown—almost black—eyes fixed on me.

As I rub at my palms I take in the room: rectangular, the walls smooth. There's a red tinge to the lights, giving the space the look of a photographic dark room. Nothing to give away a location. Just a single door.

"Where am I?"

"Another question," comes the reply from my neighbour.

"What do you expect, Kavi?" says the woman. "He's bound to be a little disorientated at first. We all were."

"And do we know any more now than we did then?" asks the man she named. Nobody rushes to answer.

Instead the woman introduces herself to me. "I'm Jane," she says, touching her chest, then thumbs over at the other man. "That's Phil."

"Philip Hall," he announces proudly, like it means something. I shrug. "Chris. Chris Warwick."

"Welcome to the party," says Phil snidely.

"So nobody knows anything about this? About why I saw someone just get fried right in front of me."

"You *saw* that?" Jane sounds shocked.

I nod. "Managed to drag my blindfold down a bit. I saw enough."

Phil gives a half laugh. "Resourceful little devil, isn't he? That'll get you a one way ticket to Hell around here, kid."

"This *is* Hell," says Jane with complete conviction.

"How long have you been here?" I ask, though it's Phil who butts in.

"Longer than you," he says.

"Then you must have seen who's holding us." I round on him. "Who did that."

Nobody says a thing.

"Oh, come on! This is ridiculous." I stand, almost putting my hands on the bars again. "You can't just kidnap a bunch of people and then—"

"Why not? Happens all the time abroad," Phil comments. "Places where *his* lot come from." He nods over at Kavi.

The dark skinned man smiles. "With one breath you betray your ignorance," is his only remark.

"We're *all* ignorant in here," Phil states.

"But how did you wind up in this place?" It's another question, and I expect Kavi to say something about that, but he doesn't. This time he asks me one of his own.

"How did *you*?"

It suddenly strikes me I don't know. I had thought I'd been out on the town or something, and just got completely smashed. But I couldn't remember a thing about the previous night, the previous *day* (what time of day is it anyway?), let alone how I ended up in this cage. "I… I think I was drugged."

"Well, *of course* you were drugged!" barks Phil. "It's how they get you here, and put you inside these things." He points at the cage.

"But why? Are they after money?"

"Looking for a ransom, that what you're thinking?" Phil grunts. "And why exactly would anyone pay money to get *you* back, Chrissie-boy? Loaded, are you?"

I hang my head. "No."

"Me either. How about you, Jane? Fitness instructor's pay suddenly gone up by a few million in the last month or so?"

"Piss off," says Jane.

Phil grins wearily. "Wish I could, sweetheart. Really wish I could."

"So what do you do?" I enquire out of mild curiosity.

"That's for me to know and for you to find out."

"He works in an estate agents," Jane informs me.

"Thanks a bunch," Phil grumbles.

"What about you?" I ask Kavi.

"Aw, who gives a shit?" Phil breaks in before he can answer. "That was in the outside world. In here you're just another plaything."

I look again at the empty cage. "Why did they do that? Burn that person up, I mean."

"Nick," Jane says quietly, her eyes glistening. "His name was Nicholas."

"They don't need to give a fucking reason," Phil explains. "They'll just come in, douse you with petrol and strike a light."

"Phil… please," begs Jane.

"Especially if you make a fuss, draw attention to yourself," he continues, ignoring her. "Just like Nick did."

It was Jane's turn to glare now, at Phil. "He didn't do anything wrong. He was just—"

"He asked one too many questions," Kavi points out, looking at me.

Phil nods in agreement. "Every time they came in, he was at

it. What the fuck did he expect?"

"Come in? Hold on…" I say, switching the subject. "So you *have* seen the people holding us then?"

Phil considers how to answer that one. "They don't exactly let us get a good look at their faces."

"I don't understand."

"You will," Kavi promises.

"Nick didn't do anything wrong," Jane continues, as if the conversation hasn't moved on at all. "It wasn't because of that—they just enjoy it." Without thinking. her hand goes to her neck and now I see the scar. It's a fresh one, still quite raw. "They enjoy hurting us."

"But why? What could they possibly gain from this? What do they want?"

"That," says Kavi, "is precisely what Nick wanted to know."

They all fall silent. After a few minutes, Jane turns to me. "Chris… Tell us about yourself. Who are you? What do you do?"

I sit back in the cage, picking at the chains. What the hey—I'm not going anywhere right now.

So I tell them. I tell them what I can remember about my life…

Interlude: Seven Years Ago

I went through the same shit as everyone else in my teens.

Struggled with my lessons, struggled with the opposite sex. I got high enough grades to take me to art school where I enjoyed a brief and actually quite enjoyable stay—able to reinvent myself for my new circle of friends—until I got thrown out for smoking dope in the toilets with Jill Stanyard. The police let me off with a caution because I told them who had supplied the joint. They informed me they'd be keeping a close eye on me, though.

My parents had split by now, and I didn't fancy living with either of them. Besides, I think they pretty much wanted to disown me after the whole college incident. So I slept on the living room floor of a friend's digs and signed on.

In my early twenties I figured I should really make an effort to do something with my life. I worked my way through any number of dead-end jobs just to earn some cash. For a while I was the guy in the street that everyone hates. You know the one, standing there with clipboard in hand. That was when I wasn't dressed up as a giant chicken, handing out leaflets about tasty battered drumsticks.

In my spare time I kept up with my art, though I'd started writing more by then: something else I'd gotten into at college. I even went to a night-class for a short while.

"Christopher, your characterisation is good. It's just your ideas that need to be worked on," the tutor told me, a pipe-smoking ex-English teacher in a tweed jacket. "They're just too... off the wall. For example, these people you keep writing about from this other dimension who manipulate the human race. The ones with the globes. I mean, *really*."

"They're just a metaphor," I tried to tell him. I thought he'd like that, being into symbolism and everything. "I guess I'm saying none of us are really in control of our own destinies."

His answer to that was, "Rubbish. We make our own choices in life, Christopher."

But we don't, do we? Some of those choices are made for us. Like if I hadn't been going to the classes I never would have met Kim, and we never would have started going out. She was there for pottery lessons and we bumped into each other in the corridor after class.

"Let me guess, ash tray?" I said, after we got chatting— referring to the object she'd been making that night.

She laughed, her eyes lighting up behind the big round glasses she wore. "Don't smoke. Actually it's supposed to be a mug."

"Ah, I see... Look, do you fancy something to eat?"

And it just went from there.

I showed Kim some of my stories and sketches; she thought I was talented, though I don't think she really got them. "You should send these off somewhere," she told me in bed one night.

"What, you mean to magazines?"

"Uh-huh."

"You think?"

"Sure. What have you got to lose? If you don't, you'll never know."

She was right. If I didn't I'd always wonder what might have been. But there was no way they were good enough, and the rejections I got back simply confirmed that. So Kim talked her boss, Mr Malone, into giving me a job in the call centre where she worked

That's about the size of it. We ate, slept, watched mindless TV and screwed. Kim and I made plans for the future, even though her parents hated my guts. Her father especially. "He's got no ambition, no prospects," I overheard him telling his daughter once. "You can do much better than him, sweetheart." They say history repeats itself, don't they?

Still, life was good for a time.

Life was normal.

Three

It isn't long before I see our jailers.

I understand now what Kavi meant, because their features are covered by hoods; cowls so large they obscure their faces. And robes that reach down almost to the ground. They look like monks belonging to some kind of religious order. *Is that it? A brotherhood dedicated to worshipping pain—inflicted upon themselves and others?* But their footwear gives them away. Heavy boots; military issue. Plus there's the merest glimpse of combat trousers as they walk.

They bring with them a replacement for 'Nick': a grey-haired old lady dragged along the floor by her flabby arms. She's blindfolded, like I was, and looks just as drugged up. They begin attaching chains to her wrists and ankles.

I exchange glances with Jane, then Phil and Kavi. The latter are begging me with their eyes not to say or do something that might cause trouble. But as I watch them open up the door of the cage and dump the woman inside, I can't hold back.

"Hey," I shout, hearing a sharp intake of breath from Jane. "Hey, I'm talking to you—you murdering bastards." It's not the smartest thing I've ever done, and I've picked a great time to act the hero, but I just can't contain my outrage any longer.

The monks pause from their labours and turn in my direction. They say nothing. Then with cold, calculating calmness they finish the job, securing the woman behind those bars.

"You cowards, hiding in those stupid outfits. Just who do you think you are?"

"Christopher," says Kavi in hushed tones that nevertheless have a hardness to them.

"Hey! I'm waiting for an answer, fuckers," I shout.

That does the trick. One walks over, the strides long and confident, robes swishing. The same swishing I heard the first time I awakened.

Head still bowed, he approaches my cage.

"You come near me and I'll…" I start, knowing it's just a hollow threat. If these people took me in the first place, then I'm no match for them now, shackled. I'm not much of a fighter anyway.

He reaches into his robes, producing a gun which he brings up level with my head.

"Serves him right," I hear Phil whisper to Jane. "I told him. Shoulda kept his big mouth shut."

I try to retreat, but the ankle chains suddenly tighten and root me to the spot. He steps closer, finger twitching on the trigger. My mouth falls open and all I can do is gape at the barrel. *Not so much of a tough guy all of a sudden, are you?* But I never claimed to be, I'm just someone who can't keep quiet. Someone like Nick.

And look what happened to him.

Barbeque.

Just when it seems there's no hope, the 'monk' turns at the last minute and points the gun at Phil. It takes him totally by surprise, as does the bang when he fires. I jump, then trace the path of the bullet. I've never seen anyone get shot before, except in the movies—and it's *so* different in real life. Phil's wide eyes screw up as the projectile hits his gut. There's a tiny explosion of blood, then a sudden flow. Phil touches the wound, his breathing fast and low. The 'monk' walks over to Phil's cage, cocking his head.

"Jesus," Phil manages. "Look what you've gone and done." His voice is thick and sounds like it's full of phlegm. The hooded figure raises the gun as if to shoot Phil again. But he doesn't; he just stands there, watching the reaction. Then, when his colleagues are about to depart from the room, he does the same, hiding the gun inside his robes once more.

It takes a long time for Phil to die.

He does his best to try and stem the bleeding, but it's like the 'monk' knew exactly where to hit him for maximum damage, yet at the same time to prolong his agony. Phil's face gradually turns white, then stony grey. All we can do is sit there, while the life-blood ebbs out of him. I think about shouting for the men to come back, for them to do something. Then I remember that it's my fault. Phil is dying because I couldn't keep my mouth fucking well shut; because I wanted answers. They've done this as a message… a warning.

Jane is crying uncontrollably, but can't take her eyes off the sight. Just like she couldn't when Nick was burning, smoking… Melting. I hear Kavi chanting something I can't understand; I think he's praying for Phil.

At the end, Phil's bladder and bowels fail him. I can smell the piss and shit. With a final wet gurgle he coughs his last breath. It sounds like he's trying to ask, "Why?"

Jane is in a state of shock, Kavi is still muttering words to help Phil's soul on its way.

I say nothing. If only I'd kept quiet a few hours ago then—

No, it's not down to me. It can't be! How would that make any sense? But the fact remains I'm still alive, and Phil is in the cage next to me—dead.

And I have to ask myself whether anything makes sense any more.

Interlude: Three Years Ago

I missed something out, probably because I've only just remembered it.

Isn't that strange? How could I have forgotten about the e-mails? You're thinking I've gone mad now, aren't you? I'm beginning to wonder myself. But trust me, this is important… I think.

I was still with Kim. Not quite ready to get hitched, but we'd talked about it, usually after too much wine at the weekend. "You know it's going to happen, don't you?" I'd say. She'd nod, but give me a look that said, 'Well, why don't you bloody well get on with it and ask me then?'

I'd been promoted at the call centre (I'd show her fucking dad who was and who wasn't ambitious!) so now I no longer had to pester people in their homes. I got others to do it for me. Kim had left there by then, and was working in a solicitor's office. The pay was better and between us we had a pretty good standard of living. I'd forgotten all about the stories I'd sent off to places, that is until one of the magazines wrote back to me saying they'd had a change of editor. Apparently my story had been languishing in a drawer for almost three years. It was only when they cleared them out that they found it. And you know what—this new editor absolutely loved it and could they please use it in a forthcoming issue?

I'd have to wait six months or more, and I wouldn't get paid much, but I didn't give a toss. Something I'd written was actually going to be published. In a real life, honest to goodness, magazine!

I told Kim when she got home from the office and we went out that night for a meal to celebrate. We fooled around when we made it back, just like we used to do in the days when we first met. It was the most tender and intimate sex I'd ever had in my life. I don't know about Kim, but I can definitely recommend getting something published as an aphrodisiac.

We both called in sick the next day. It was only partially a lie, as we should never have finished that last bottle of red. It took till about noon for both of us to feel up to surfacing. I switched on my computer in the spare room and downloaded my mails while I went off to use the loo. When I walked back in, I saw a load of spam had come through. Usually the filters dealt with all that, but they must have been on the fritz.

Mails were coming in from people like Chick Dalke, Rodney Bunter, Janis A. Ohio, trying to get me to buy anything from sex pills to replica watches. Some of them just didn't make any sense at all.

'Here's the lube you neeeeeeeed,' said one. 'Let it glide with pride. This oil will make it feeed, quicker than you can blink.' Another was just a random list of words: 'Eminent mandrake accost plasma blizzard corruption nordhoff hyena locomotory genus militate neonatal…' Pure nonsense.

"Well, you definitely don't need any of *that* stuff," said Kim over my shoulder, pointing at one ad that promised to give the woman in my life sexual ecstasy. 'Take me beyond my limits,' said the woman standing there, finger crooked. "She can wait her turn." Kim began nibbling my earlobe, obviously still in the mood after last night.

I allowed myself to get dragged off back to bed, but all the time Kim ground away on top of me my mind was elsewhere. Something in those mails, especially the nonsense ones, was nagging at me. What did it mean? How had they made their way through now, why did they continue to come to millions of people…? The rational part of my mind was telling me the mails were corrupted because they'd multiplied until the original message was no longer comprehensible. But the other part— that dreamt up the story which had just been accepted by the magazine—was telling me something else. What if the nonsense was just a smokescreen? What if there was something important I was missing in those mails?

"Mmmm… Oh yes," murmured Kim as she lowered, angling herself so that the sensations she felt intensified. Her eyes were closed as she impaled herself on me, her moans growing louder, the creaking of the bed in tune to the rhythm of her hips. The image of that half-naked woman flitted into my mind, a construct of pixels, a fantasy someone had thought up to sucker people.

Then, suddenly, other images of women intruded, pages from some old magazine.

"Take me... Take me beyond my limits," whispered Kim. I wasn't sure whether she was joking, using the phrase from the woman's speech bubble as a gag. "Take me... Take me," she repeated. I pushed her onto her back, holding her by the wrists, and began to ram into her hard. Her moans reached fever pitch as I thrust in right to the hilt, again and again, making both of us raw. "Harder! Oh God, harder! Hurt me... hurt me!"

Let it glide with pride... Make it feeed, quicker than you can blink.

Pleasure mixed with pain, creating something totally unique. The orgasm, when it came, was unlike anything I'd ever experienced. I felt Kim quivering beneath me as I held onto her. But it wasn't until I looked down again that I saw she was quivering with fear, red finger marks indenting her skin. She rolled over, sobbing into the pillow.

I reached out a hand to touch her shoulder; she shrugged it off.

"Baby...?"

Kim turned back and I saw anger in her face this time. "What the hell got into you? That hurt, Chris. That *really* hurt!"

"But you said... I thought—"

"What? That I was enjoying it? Didn't you hear me telling you to stop?" She was practically screaming the words.

I shook my head.

"Having too much of a good time, were you? What's next, handcuffs? Whipping? Gimp masks?"

"No... You know I'm not into all that stuff."

Her look said she didn't know me at all. "Just leave me alone, would you. Leave me the fuck alone." Kim buried her head into the pillow again.

Frowning, I climbed out of bed. I had no idea what had just happened, but I did know I'd hurt the person I loved more than anything. What *had* got into me? I honestly had no clue. The images in my head, the words Kim had been saying... Something about those mails.

I returned to the computer in the spare room, which had flipped to the screensaver. Nudging the mouse brought up the spam and I examined those emails once more.

I was so transfixed I didn't hear Kim get up and get dressed, and only realised she'd left the flat when I heard the door slam. Later I found the note she'd left me saying she'd gone to her folks to stay. She'd even packed some of her clothes.

Kim returned the following week, but only after I'd left many pleading messages on her mobile. "I swear I don't know what happened," I tried to explain. "Please come back. I need you."

She finally relented, in spite of her mother and father's protests. But things were never the same. It was a long time before she would let me anywhere near her, saying that she just wanted the old Chris back, the person she'd fallen in love with.

I wanted to tell her that it *was* still me, but we both knew that would have been a lie. I'd had a revelatory moment that day, and I was certain it had something to do with the mails. What I never told her was that I'd saved them, and disabled the filters permanently so that I'd get more. I studied them, searching for something...

Strangely, it was while I wasn't looking at all that I spotted the answer. Dropping to sleep in the chair, staring at the computer one night, another batch of mails flooded in. Kim was downstairs watching TV, on her own, as she did most nights. I clicked on the first mail and saw this text, suddenly drawn to certain letters:

'I struck some small cork after your ill sky, which bade uniformly. Its narrow box around that knowledge, bitter, necessary pin, wet stone shelf interbred. They slunk, afterwards, only, I hanged her hard operation beyond his important cloud. Which reran often, acid reading remade of this need?'

I rubbed my sore eyes, blinking. Random coincidence? The

letters just happened to make up that sentence? But not the placing of the full stops, separating out each word so there could be no mistake.

'They watch and wait'.

I checked through the other mails I'd stored, now that I'd broken the code. I saw it again and again. Sometimes it would be down the sides—to the left or the right of justified text. Sometimes it was diagonally across, like a wordsearch puzzle. Other times, like the first one, simply embedded.

"My God," I said to myself, clicking on another incoming mail.

The computer froze. Had to happen sooner or later, a virus of some kind. I moved the cursor and nothing happened. I pressed Ctrl, Alt and Delete together. No task manager box came up. I found myself jabbing hard at one of the keys over and over again.

Harder! Oh God harder…

I looked down. It was the Ctrl key. Ctrl…

Control?

"I'm going to bed, now. You can do what you want." The voice startled me and I jumped. Turning, I saw Kim standing in the doorway wearing her 'keep your hands to yourself' pyjamas.

"What…? Oh, yeah, sure." I turned back to the dead screen. She sighed, but didn't bother looking again.

I just stared at the blankness, wondering quite what I'd stumbled onto. The virus behind the virus. One that ensured no computer would ever work for me again.

It didn't come as a surprise when, a few weeks later, the magazine who had accepted my story told me that they were folding and couldn't publish it after all.

"It's such a sad thing," the woman told me, almost in tears down the line. "The editor threw himself in front of a tube train. There was no warning, nothing anyone could have done."

"No," I said, the phone falling from my grasp. "I don't think anyone could."

Four

The new addition's name is Patty.

They take her blindfold off at the same time they come and clear out Phil's body, wheeling it from the room on a trolley. This time I keep quiet as the men in robes do their work. The old woman watches, but doesn't say a word either. I think she may be catatonic.

Once the 'monks' have gone again, it is Jane who talks to her, eventually coaxing out a name.

"That man," Patty says, "he was dead, wasn't he?"

"Killed... shot," I inform her. "By the men that brought you here."

"Those same people in the hoods and cloaks."

Jane nods.

"Oh sweet Lord." Patty's voice trembles. She has a kindly face, the youthfulness shining out and belying her years. I feel an immediate affinity with Patty. She has that look on her face I must have had when I first arrived: a combination of denial and confusion. The next words out of her mouth confirm this. "Why did they kill him? What do they want with me?"

"I wish we could answer your questions," Kavi says, "but we are as much in the dark as you."

"Do you remember how you got here?" I ask.

Patty shakes her head. "No, wait... I think I was at home. I remember I was feeding Mr Vickers." She smiles thinly and adds, "My cat. Then... Then there was a knock at the door. I went to see who it was."

"And..."

"I... don't know, it's all so muddled. I can't remember much after that."

"Jesus." I bang my fist into my hand; a humourless imitation of Robin from the old *Batman* series. "Please try to think."

"I'm sorry," she replies, gazing at me. "My memory's not what it was at the best of times."

"Look, it's obvious they don't want us to know," Jane says to me. "None of us can remember, no matter how hard we try."

"It is futile striving to know the unknowable," Kavi concludes.

I snort. "Right. Is that why you pray? I saw you when Phil was dying."

Kavi slowly closes then opens his eyes. "Praying does not reveal the unknowable to me, it simply puts me in touch with my God. He hears my plea. But at the same time I do not *demand* anything from Him."

"No, because he bloody well won't answer you, will he?"

"The words of a Godless man, am I right?"

I say nothing.

"I accept what is and what must be," Kavi answers as enigmatically as ever. "Most men do not."

That's directed at me. "Well, I don't accept that there's nothing I can do to get out of here. Nothing to do but watch and—"

"Wait?" Kavi finishes for me.

"T-That's right." I turn back to Patty. "Can you think of any reason why you might have been kidnapped?"

She shakes her head. "None at all. I'm nothing special, young man."

"Maybe that's just it," Jane interrupts. "Maybe we've been looking at this from the wrong angle. Have you ever thought that they've chosen us simply because we're ordinary? Because we won't be missed? Heaven knows nobody would give a toss if I vanished off the face of the Earth. I haven't seen my ex in years and I moved recently so I don't have any close friends in the area. How about the rest of you?"

"My wife and small son," Kavi informs her, a faraway look in his eye. "They would miss me."

"My husband passed away many years ago, but there's my daughter," Patty says. "And my little grandson, though he's probably too young to remember his old Gran if something should…" Her eyes begin to moisten.

I pause to think, who would miss me? Who would actually care if I died right here in this cage like some kind of lab rat?

Before I have too much time to mull it over, our food is brought in. Some kind of brown slop in a bowl with a spoon. It isn't until one of the hooded figures draws closer with the stuff that I realise how incredibly hungry I am. I probably haven't had anything to eat in well over forty-eight hours, though time has a way of becoming meaningless in this room. Our chains tighten as the cages are undone and the bowls placed inside.

When the cages are locked again, and the 'monks' have departed, our bonds loosen. Jane and Kavi reach for their bowls and begin to spoon up the slop into their mouths. It's obvious they've eaten at this restaurant before. Patty just sits and stares at the offering they've placed in her cage.

I hunker over the bowl, sniffing. It smells distinctly meaty. When I push the spoon around there are chunks of something in the broth.

"You should eat," Jane encourages me, "before they come and take it away again. You never know if you're going to get another meal."

"You mean they'd starve us?" I ask.

"It would not be the first time," Kavi says. "Imagine having to eat while someone else is wasting away. That is true torture, my friend. For you and for them."

I raise a spoonful and my stomach rumbles. "But… what is it?"

"If we ask do you think they'd tell us?" Jane had a point.

I bring the spoon to my lips. Isn't half bad—a bit like beef stew. Greedily, I tuck in.

"Patty, you should eat too," Jane calls across, getting to the bottom of her bowl.

"I can't face it," she replies honestly.

"You need to keep your strength up," Jane insists.

Patty pouts. "What, because I'm a frail old lady?"

"No, I didn't mean—"

Patty folds her arms, more determined than ever not to eat.

"This is my first time as well," I say. "But, really, it's not as bad as it looks. Go on, take a—"

Jane, who has just put her last spoonful into her mouth, begins to cough. At first I think she's choking, but it's more than that. Her hands are clutching at her belly. She falls over, doubling up. "Awwwhhhh!"

"Jane... Jane, what is it?" A stupid question, and one she's in no position to answer. But then this is me all over, I'm beginning to realise: stupid.

Jane's convulsing, and she brings her fingers up to her mouth—a vain effort to stick them down her throat. But before she can try and make herself sick, another stab of pain strikes and she curls up into a ball, hugging her abdomen tightly.

I place my hands on the bars of my cage, forgetting for a moment that they might be live. Nothing happens, so I shake them, causing the cage to rattle as well. There's no hope of escape, let alone helping Jane, but doing *something* makes me feel slightly better.

"She's been poisoned," Kavi says, staring down at his own bowl.

Patty places her hands over her ears as Jane cries out again. The younger woman is kicking out, her feet hitting the bars. Her teeth are gritted, but foamy saliva sprays through them, drooling onto the cage floor. Jane's eyes are turning bright red, blood vessels exploding in the whites—and she's looking right at me as if expecting me to do something.

Her body is jerking all over the place, and at some point her tongue has forced its way out through her teeth. I wince as she chomps down on it, the wet end severing completely and flopping to the base of her cage on strings of spit and muscle.

Her exposed arms are breaking out in welts, huge balls that fill with pus, like some kind of time-elapsed film of a disease. Jane's face, too, once pretty, is ruined by whatever's ravaging her body—whatever they put in the stew. I know it shouldn't even enter my mind, but I can't help wondering if they've done the same to all of us.

You only had a taste, though, remember? Just a taste...

How can I think about that when Jane is suffering like this? The lumps forming on her brow have closed one eye completely shut. She's scratching at the raised bits, raking it with her nails as the deformed skin tightens. Jane attempts to speak, but the ragged end of her tongue is swelling—blocking her airway—so all we can hear are disgusting gurglings. She's like some creature out of a sci-fi movie, transforming from human being into something else. It's a blessing when she can't breathe any more, and as she collapses onto the cage floor, her skin tears, leaking in many places.

I look from her to Kavi, then to Patty. None of us can quite believe what we've just seen. But already I can see a hardness in our new guest, the shock less than when they wheeled away Phil. The same is happening with me, I suppose. This is the third person I've seen die here. I don't think it will be the last.

With a resigned and frustrated grunt, I hurl the rest of my bowl at the bars of my cage. "Let us out of here!" I shout at the ceiling, at the walls. "You bastards, let us out!"

Interlude: One Year and Five Months Ago…

As you can imagine, Kim didn't stick around for very long once I started to suspect the truth.

One day I came back from work (I was just about holding on to the job) and she'd packed her bags again, this time everything. And this time for good. She didn't even leave me a note, and I didn't bother ringing. It was all a sham anyway. I'm not just talking about our relationship, but things in general: life, people, work, all of it.

I was beginning to notice the signs everywhere I went. It was like someone had taken off a blindfold and allowed me to see— or I'd pulled it off myself, struggling to uncover what was right in front of my eyes. Ripping down the illusion of the everyday; not just walking on the cracks in the pavement, but getting down on my hands and knees and putting my eye up against them.

It didn't go unnoticed at the call centre. One day my boss, Malone, called me in. I stood there being chastised like a naughty schoolkid.

"I just don't understand it, Christopher. You have… *had* a future here with us. What went wrong? I'd say it was trouble at home with Kim but I know this started before that."

"What do you know about me and Kim?" I snapped. Already I could picture my hands around his throat, squeezing.

"We're still friends. We keep in touch."

"I'll bet you do." Now they were squeezing harder.

"What's that supposed to mean?"

I shook my head to clear it. "Look, it doesn't matter. You want my resignation, you got it. None of this means anything anyway."

Malone sniffed. "Obviously, judging by the smell of your breath. You're not even trying to hide it, are you? The drinking?"

"How can I put this politely," I replied, fighting back the image of strangling him again. "Fuck right off."

"Do me a favour, don't let the door hit you on the way out."

I didn't. But I do remember saying something like, "And you can all get fucked as well!" to the other employees in the centre. They were still asleep, while I had begun to wake.

It took some time to prove what I already knew. That this phenomenon, the code I'd cracked, was everywhere if you just chose to look.

I'd walk down the high street and see it on billboards, supposedly promoting the latest cars or perfumes, but in reality… I remember just standing and staring at one poster for most of the day. The advert showed a picture of a man with a tank-top holding up a bowl of cereal, while a woman with a bob-cut was standing behind him beaming, ready to dip her own spoon in. Nothing suspicious whatsoever.

But the more I examined it, the more I saw the intent behind those eyes. They were saying something much more than: 'We love the new honey flavour'.

Several people stopped and asked me what I was looking at.

"Can't you see it?" I said to them.

"See what?"

"The message behind the message?"

"All I can see is a guy with a bowl of cereal."

So it went on. I'd warn them to walk away before I started

shouting. Some did, some didn't. Some asked where the hidden cameras were, and I had to laugh at that. I came to the conclusion that they couldn't see past the surface because they didn't *want* to; they were just protecting themselves. Jesus, how much simpler would my life have been if I'd never found out?

I scoured the newspapers day after day. The celebrity gossip columns, the sports pages, the hard factual stories about wars abroad. Especially those. Even in the horoscopes it was there: 'Watch out for overspending, Pisces... Don't let work pressures get you down, Virgo... You have received some important information, Aquarius, what you choose to do with it is up to you.'

Because the internet was now forbidden—a two-way mirror that I didn't dare use anymore—I visited libraries, museums, seats of learning. I found the message again and again in encyclopaedias, in the ideas of famous scholars. Philosophers such as Nietzsche, Aristotle, Wittgenstein, Locke, Kant and so many others hinted at it, though they had no idea they were so close to the truth.

In the greatest works of literature I saw hidden signs. The plays of Shakespeare, the poems of Byron, the novels of Dickens. And don't even get me started on parables in the Bible!

But in works of art, also, it was as plain as the nose on your face: the key in every brushstroke, every chip with the hammer and chisel. People like the Surrealists came the closest to breaking it. You think Dali's 'Lobster Telephone' is just for effect, or Magritte's men with bowler hats and pictures of pipes? *Ceci n'est pas une pipe.* You're damned right it's not, René.

Architecture? Sure. The Doric, Ionic and the Corinthian screamed it out, the towers and castles of the Gothic era, the reflective surfaces of the Lloyd building... Every single one of them, if you took the trouble to look, to *really* look as I did, contained some element of the message.

Let us not forget film and television. Name your favourite movie, it's there in every line of dialogue, every scene, every jump cut or special effects sequence. Charlie Chaplin's tramp, God love him, Rhett Butler and Scarlett O'Hara's kiss, Rita Hayward in *that* dress, the shark in *Jaws*, the aliens in fucking *Independence*

Day for Christ sakes! And the writers, producers and directors behind them, all unable to see the result of what they'd done. That not only was their stamp on the work, but another as well.

Should I try to make others see? Could they? *Would* they? In the end I chose to do what most would have done in my place, armed with the knowledge I had.

I decided to get drunk. (See, like father like son. Kim's dad was right after all.)

I took myself off at night and drank my way through the savings account Kim and I had set up, hitting bar after bar. There you'd find me, with a scotch or vodka, in the corner, observing the mating rituals and ruckuses. It didn't matter whether it was a nightclub, wine bar or just some downbeat pub, it was all the same.

Once or twice I'd cause a scene, just to see what happened.

"Don't any of you fucking get it? You really don't, do you? You're all being used, manipulated!"

It would usually end in me being thrown out by a very large bouncer.

Around this time I began to dabble with drugs again, too. I figured it would help me to forget, might even make life worth living once more.

I was wrong.

Some of the trips I had... In one I was communicating with different coloured lights: bright reds and yellows, greens and purples. Each colour had its own personality and I passed a pleasant evening in conversation until black came along, absorbing the others.

In another I was lost in a forest of bones, human bones—and beneath my feet I trampled human skeletons into the ground as I ran, trying to get away from something behind me.

But one in particular struck a chord. I felt myself rising up out of my body and travelling through the stars, until space itself turned white and the pinpricks of light turned black. There I saw a city, with living towers and minarets, surrounded by volcanoes that spat fire—burning white fire—periodically. The snaking streets of this place, connected by juddering bridges and pulsating conduits, were labyrinthine in design. The creatures who inhabited the buildings wore clothes that seemed to be a part of their own bodies: fleshy, covered in veins, protective cowls covering their features. Cowls that glowed a strange azure colour.

Beneath the ground of this city was a huge eye—liquid blue. Swimming in this were all the souls who had ever been and ever would be; floaters in the eye, dispelled whenever it blinked. It looked right at me, that eye. Right *into* me.

I woke from that one in the Emergency Room, towel wrapped around me. I was soaking wet.

"He's finally coming around. Whatever he took was really strong stuff!" This was a doctor who was flashing a torch into my eyes. He clicked his fingers to the side of me and when I reacted, he sighed with relief. "How people can let themselves get into this state, I'll never know."

"How… where…?" I breathed.

"You were found in the lake, guy. Could easily have drowned if that courting couple hadn't come across you. You're lucky to be alive."

I didn't *feel* lucky. "Listen… listen to me. My story… I have to tell you my story!"

"Yeah, yeah." He grinned. "They all say that. Listen, why don't you take it easy for a minute." The doctor pushed me back, about to flash the light in my eyes again. "I just want to take another look at—"

"You don't understand. None of you do. They watch and—"

A nurse appeared with a huge needle and handed it to the doctor. I took one look at that and started to struggle.

"Easy now. This is for your own good. God, after the crap you put into your own body tonight, you'd think that—"

I lashed out, knocking him sideways, then pushed the nurse backwards. I stumbled from the bed, tipping over a tray of instruments. I vaguely remember shoving a few people aside in my hurry to reach the door.

But I made it, out into the dark.

I ran, just like I did through that forest of bones. When I was exhausted, I hid away in a deserted area of town, in an old

50

abandoned factory the derelicts sometimes use.

I sat there in the blackness, knees up to my chest, knowing that I'd been seen now for sure.

That They would do everything in Their power to catch me and—

Well, then They would silence me for good.

Five

Jane's replacement is already well on the way to death when they bring him in.

The door opens as we're discussing what happened to her— Kavi and I can at least agree on some kind of biological weapon— and the 'monks' shove the man inside. He is stripped to the waist with his hands bound behind his back. In his mid-fifties perhaps, with long silver-grey hair and a trimmed beard, he has been worked on outside. For starters his eye is missing, in its place just a huge cavity. When he's pushed to his knees I see two fingers are gone on his right hand, and the thumb of his left. There are marks across his back where a belt or something has been used on him. Scars on his chest, a bit like those Jane tried to hide.

I look at Kavi and nod towards the newcomer. He shakes his head, telling me silently that he's never seen this guy before. Patty touches her fingers to her lips, face as white as a shroud. I think she's finally grasping the fact that this could be her soon, and we can't do a blessed thing about it. But the more I look at her face, the more I recognise not just the look, but the features. There's something so desperately familiar and I wish I could work out what.

The new guy looks completely out of it, ribs bruised purple where they've beaten him. One of the 'monks' kicks him in the direction of the cage he's about to occupy.

Roll up, roll up, roll up... For incineration, bleeding to death from a belly wound, emaciation and poisoning.

The men in robes manhandle him into Jane's cage, which has

only been vacant a short while. As he slumps inside and they undo one lot of shackles, only to replace them with those inside the cage, I see burn marks on the soles of his feet. He's really been through the wringer.

With a clang of the cage door, our jailors leave again. The man rolls around groaning.

"Hey!" I call. "Hey you! Can you hear me?"

"What are you doing?" Patty asks, biting her nails.

"He's been out there." I point to the door. "He's seen what's outside of here. If we're going to try and escape—"

"Escape?" she says, a little too loudly for my liking.

"Christopher, how many more times: there is no escape from here," says Kavi hanging his head. "Nicholas, Philip and now Jane... Dozens more before you arrived."

"I am not going to sit here waiting to buy it on some sadomasochistic production line," I snap. "Especially when I don't know why."

"People are born, people live, people die—all the time," Kavi points out. "How many of *them* know why?"

"Bet that God of yours knows," I retort, the sarcasm dripping from my voice. "Now why don't you—"

"H-He's right." The voice is barely a whisper, but it cuts through our babble like a blade. The man they brought in is leaning up on one elbow. "T-There's no escaping this."

Eyebrows knitting together, I grab the bars of my cage once more, again forgetting they could be charged. It's just in my nature to rage against captivity. "What are you talking about? There *has* to be a way out. How many guards are there?"

He just laughs, then begins to wheeze like an asthmatic in need of an inhaler.

"Tell me! Tell me anything you can!" I'm beginning to lose patience; I don't give a shit what state he's in.

"Be dead soon, me, and so will all of you lot."

I shake my head. "I don't give up that easily."

"You... you will eventually, boy. We all do."

I freeze. There's something about that voice, I've heard it before. The man is cleaner than he was the first time we met, though not that much older.

I'm not going back! You hear me? Never!

"You're The Monster," I say.

"What?"

"You know this man?" asks Kavi.

I nod.

"How?"

"When I was a kid, I think. It's all a bit hazy…"

"Why did you call him a monster?" Patty chirps up.

The man in the cage wheezes again. "I'm Dixon. Folks call me Dixon," he says, as if to prove he's human.

"I'm not sure," I tell Patty. "But I think he knows more about all this than any of us."

The man shakes his head, then looks away. "No, not me. I don't know nothin'."

"*Liar!*" If I could get to him right now, I'd force the information out. Then I stop and look at his wounds again. He's been through enough. "Look, just tell us what's on the other side of that door—how we can get out. You got out before, I know you did. I remember that much."

"You're saying that this man escaped and was brought back?" Kavi rubs his chin.

"Tell me!" I demand again, ignoring Kavi.

The man looks around him as if following the trail of a fly. "Can't. They… They watch."

"And They wait?" I state matter of factly. "There are cameras in here, aren't there? They're watching us right now."

"They're *always* watching us," hisses the man. "Night and day, day and night. *You are the one!*" He sings this last bit.

"The man has clearly lost his mind." Kavi's pacing up and down in the confines of his cage.

"Show yourself! Come on!" I'm suddenly shouting. "Let us see you—we know you're there!"

The door opens and two of the 'monks' rush in. It's almost as if they've been waiting on the other side, ready to move whenever there's trouble.

"Hey!" I shout again.

"Christopher…" There's a definite warning in Kavi's voice.

"Here! Come over here, I want to talk to you." I never have been one for learning from my mistakes. I rattle my bars and it succeeds in halting them. But instead of going for me, they make their way over to Kavi's cage instead. One of them reaches inside their robes.

"No, not again. Hey, over here! Me, it's me who wants to talk to you!" The bars of the cage are suddenly crackling with electricity that knocks me backwards. At the same time Kavi's shackles tighten, hoisting him up and backwards so that he is slammed against the rear of the cage: his body forms a perfect X.

Shaking my head, I see that it's not a pistol they've taken out this time, but some kind of thick noose on the end of a metal stick.

Effortlessly, they loop the open end around Kavi's head, around his neck, and with a twist they tighten it. The muscles of Kavi's arms bulge, but the shackles binding him allow no leeway. Another twist of the handle and his mouth is wide open, he's fighting for breath. They're garrotting him, with each twist of the handle tightening the pressure on his throat. Beads of sweat pour down Kavi's face, as the bonds are pulled yet tighter. Just as another twist comes, the chains yank his shoulders out of their sockets with a loud crack.

"No! No, you fuckers—*me!* I'm the one you want!" My eyes are wet with tears. This shouldn't be happening. I shouldn't be seeing this. I hear Patty's wailing from the other cage; there's not a sound from Dixon.

And, as Kavi's limbs are torn out of their sockets, his neck broken by the noose, he mouths the words: "Pray for me."

I would if I could.

It is only now that the cameras reveal themselves, the ones I suspected were in the room all along. They detach themselves from the ceiling, round like the cages and suspended by power cables. They look like miniature CCTV cams you might find in the middle of shopping precincts. Four in total, one for each prisoner, each with a single circular lens in the middle.

The nearest one descends to my level. It stares at me and I

wonder who I'm staring back at, through that lens.

"I *will* get out of here, I promise you. I'll get out. Then I'm going to come for you."

Big words, with nothing to back them up.

The camera just gazes at me in silence.

Interlude: Five Days Ago

I went on the run.

Doesn't that sound cool, like something out of a Quinn Martin production? Every week a different adventure, helping people put right what once went wrong then moving on again, the noble hero.

What a load of crap.

It was hard on the streets. I had no money—I'd lost my wallet during the incident in the Emergency Room, and anyway my card could be traced (also there wasn't much left in my account). I couldn't afford for anyone to know where I was or what I was doing.

I headed North, away from the towns and cities. I figured there'd be less scrutiny in the wide, open spaces, little realising that a stranger often sticks out like a sore thumb. The other drawback was people had a tendency to notice you begging for money, too. But I had to eat, collect other 'materials'. Outside supermarkets was the best bet, until I was inevitably moved on by security staff. I'm not too proud to admit that I stole. How else was I meant to survive? To carry out my plan?

I was aware that They could track me down at any time, but what gave me the edge was *knowing* about Them. Once you do, it becomes a lot easier to live off the grid.

Eventually I had to stop running and gather everything together. The evidence I would need to try—maybe—and convince someone. By this time I was beginning to find it very lonely carrying the burden.

I discovered a deserted cabin in the woods, a hunting lodge

that hadn't been used in years. It was practically gutted, partly burnt, but suited my needs perfectly.

I set up shop there, compiling my notes by candlelight at night and catching the odd fish or small animal to eat in the day. I know what you're thinking: Me—Grizzly Adams. They don't exactly go together, do they? But I did all right. I holed up long enough to put everything together. A case that even Perry Mason would balk at going up against. I felt like I was finally making progress, getting my head around things...

Nobody could have been more surprised than I was when *she* turned up.

Kim.

She knocked on the door out of common courtesy, but it was open anyway. As I had been that day on the computer, I was so caught up in what I was doing, I didn't look up until she was virtually inside.

"Christopher... Chris, is that you?"

I frowned at the figure standing before me: an hallucination? A bad flashback, the drugs having their revenge? But she was as real as I was.

"How... How did you find me?"

It was her turn to frown. "*You* called my mobile number, left a message. I was so pleased to hear from you!"

I laughed. "I don't even have a phone anymore."

"But you must have. Oh God, Chris, what's happened to you?" She walked further in, looking at the walls where I'd pinned pieces of paper or drawn on the wood in chalk, then her eyes settled on me again. I was sitting on the floor in the middle of more papers; I'd been furiously writing before Kim came in. It had been months since I'd seen myself in any kind of mirror, so had no idea what she was seeing. I knew my hair was long and I'd grown a beard... I was still wearing the old clothes I'd run off in that first night, but had managed to snag an overcoat from a toilet cubicle (the owner had left it on the back of the door). Christ, though, what a mess I must have looked.

"Kim, listen, if They know where I am, if *They* left that message, then I don't have a lot of time. It isn't exactly how I wanted to do this, but I suppose it's appropriate that you should be the first to see. The first other than me, that is."

"Chris, where have you been all this time? How did you get all the way up here? People have been looking for you."

One of my eyebrows arched. "People, what people?"

"The police, mainly. They were waiting for me when I got to hospital the night you vanished."

"What the fuck were you doing *there*?" My tone was harsh and I immediately regretted it.

"My number was still down as point of contact if anything should… They said you were on drugs, said you'd hurt people."

I stood, letting the papers pool around me. "I couldn't let them take me away—didn't know who to trust."

"Why? Because of all… this?" Kim glanced around the room again.

I started towards her and she backed off. "It's okay, look, I figured it all out."

"What? All I see are drawings of ellipses, coloured in blue."

I nodded. "It's an eye. It's a symbol. We're being watched, Kim. Maybe even now, I'm not sure."

"I-I don't understand."

"Nobody knows it, but I swear it's the truth. Our lives are being contr—" I hesitated, blinked, then said, "Being *manipulated*. The clues are everywhere, in everything. It's not exactly like my stories, but—"

"Your stories?"

"You remember, I almost got one published. But I don't think they could let it get out into the open. Even though it was fiction, it might have given people ideas."

"Yes, of course I remember. But they were just made up, you said so yourself."

"I did, but I know now they were my own way of dealing with what's been going on. I struck on something, Kim, and didn't even realise it."

She shook her head. "Chris, there's something wrong with you. That night, the doctors told me—"

"I knew it. I just knew it! Don't you see, they'd tell you

anything to make you think I was cracking up."

"The… the people who are watching us, right?" Kim didn't sound convinced.

"Not people, exactly. Nostradamus almost had it right," I told her. "He said gods would arrive in the form of humans, and be the cause of great conflict. But They're not here at all, They never were. I don't know exactly what They are, something our brains probably can't cope with… I do know They stay well out of it, wind us up and let us go—like clockwork toys. They… 'encourage' us to batter each other, emotionally and physically, and get off on it! Can you believe that? They don't like to get their own hands dirty; it's like reality TV or something. But They *need* us to be damaged, it… empowers them."

"Chris, you're really scaring me."

I took another couple of steps towards her, holding out my hands so she could see I meant no harm. "I've been able to see the patterns for some time now. They have a hand in everything we do—the arts, politics, advertising—every fucking thing, Kim!"

"What are you talking about? How can art cause pain, conflict?" I could tell by her face that she didn't get it.

"What do we do when we create something? We argue over its worth. It creates divisions, even on a small scale. We fight wars sometimes because we can't agree on the fundamental principles of life, of religion, of anything! While they sit back and just keep cranking up the tension. They *make* us hurt each other, Kim—just like that time I hurt you." I bent down and grabbed a handful of those papers on the floor, shoving them in her direction. "Here, see, it's all in my notes, my research. It isn't fiction this time—it's fact!"

Her mouth moved as she read the first line. "'They watch and wait.'"

I nodded. "Exactly."

"No," she said, giving me the paper back, "that's all it says, Chris, over and over again: 'They watch and wait.'"

"What? Here, give me that!" I snatched it from her and looked at the words I'd written. Hours and hours of painstaking work, thoughts, hypotheses, all somehow wiped out. "This can't be…

How have they done this?" I looked at her. "They must have implanted it subliminally, not *allowed me* to write what I thought I was writing."

Kim was nodding, but she was backing up towards the door. "Subliminal… yes, I see now."

I ran at her, grabbing her arms. "I'm telling you the truth. It's all out there, if you only choose to see."

Kim tried to break loose, but I wouldn't allow her. "Let go of me, Chris. I came here to help you. They said you might be dangerous but—"

"Who? Who said that?" I shook her. "Their acolytes? The ones who serve, even though they don't know it?"

Kim finally broke free and fell backwards, crying.

"You've brought them here, haven't you?"

She continued to cry, just as she had into her pillow.

"Why else would you come?"

"Because you *asked* me to!" she screamed. "Because even after everything, after all this time, I still love you!"

I stood there, looking down on her.

"Nobody makes us hurt each other. We do it to ourselves, Chris! There's nobody watching or waiting, nobody out there controlling any of us. Controlling anything. We. Do. It. To. Ourselves!" She said each word individually, to give it impact.

I swallowed before answering. "Then how do you explain that?" I pointed down at the ground, the way the papers had fallen on the floor.

Kim rose, eyes flicking between me and the white sheets. They'd fallen in the shape of a giant eye, perfect in every way. She said nothing.

"They're coming for me, aren't they?"

"Chris, they're going to *help* you." Even after all this, Kim still couldn't accept it.

"No-one can do that." I made to pass her, then stopped. I leaned in for a kiss and, as disgusting as I must have looked, she kissed me back. "I'm sorry," I said, breaking off. "I have to go."

Kim didn't try to stop me. It might have been because she knew the authorities were already on their way, but I like to think it had something to do with realising the truth.

I can still picture her there, standing in the doorway, looking back at me as I disappeared into the trees.

Six

I suspect Dixon died during the night, or what passes for night here—a dimming of already pretty dim lights.

When I wake, I see he's not moving, and he doesn't answer me when I repeatedly call him. He's had enough, finally given up. We now have another cell-mate, another woman in Kavi's cage. She's unconscious as well, but I figure she's not dead yet or they wouldn't have put her in here. What would be the point? The cameras—which have vanished now, but I know are still around—wouldn't be able to catch our reactions then. Wouldn't be able to savour the agony on the faces of the torture victims.

Patty is not much conversation. I find myself missing Kavi, even with his irritating ways. I wonder absently if the new woman will be any more company? She's laying with her back to me at the moment; all I can see is her blonde hair, much lighter than Jane's. She's not blindfolded, at least—I can tell that much.

For about the millionth time I wish I could get out of this fucking cell! There has to be a way.

It's at this point the woman, obviously waking from a drug-induced sleep, begins to stir. She rolls over, the blonde hair falling across her face in curls. She brings a hand up and rubs at that face, moving the curls to one side.

I take in a sharp breath. No, it can't be. "Mum…?"

The woman moans something, not quite with it yet. But it's definitely her; my mother, who ran off with the guy from the bookmakers all that time ago.

They're going after my family now?

Who will I see in here next, who will they torture just to film my reaction to it? I can't let them harm her, not like they've done with Phil, Jane, Kavi… I can see visions of the terrible things they might do to her. Pour acid onto her face, perhaps? Slit her nose open with a knife? Carve her up like those roasts she used to cook on a Sunday.

The more I stare the more I realise something is wrong with this picture. Don't get me wrong, it's Mum—I'd recognise her anywhere. Except... except she doesn't seem to have aged since I last saw her. As she pushes herself up, the shackles preventing her from going far, I see her face clearly for the first time. It's the same as it was when I was ten, maybe even younger. No lines like I noticed the last time I went to see her a few years back (I just couldn't stand that idiot she lived with).

"Mum?" I say it louder, hopefully loud enough to bring her back to the here and now. She looks at me blankly; no recognition. "Mum, it's me. It's Chris." She just gazes at me.

"A... Alice, is that you?" Patty's voice startles me, possibly because I've never heard it so frightened and excited at the same time—not even when she was fearing for her own life. Alice? That's my mother's name. Alice Warwick (nee Harper). But how could... Patty must know her, live in the same area, on the same street?

No.

As I look from one face to the other, it's so obvious now I could cry. The same nose, the same mouth. How many of us ever study our parents' faces? *Really* study them? If we did we might well see mirrors of ourselves reflected there. I was always told I had my father's chin, Mum's eyes. But she in turn had inherited features from *her* mother.

"My husband passed away many years ago, but there's my daughter, and my little grandson, though he's probably too young to remember his old Gran..."

Patty... Patricia. Patricia Harper! A woman I barely knew, who died when I was only small. I'd seen a few photos growing up, of course, but... Christ Almighty!

"Mum," says 'Alice', parroting my words. "What are you doing here? Where am I?" A look of complete and utter shock comes across her face. "You're... You're dead. You died when I was... Oh my God, that's it, isn't it? I'm dead, too! And I'm in" Mum looks down at the manacles on her wrists and ankles, at the bars surrounding her.

I know exactly what she's thinking: Jane said it once. This *is* Hell. And we're all being punished for something.

Only I don't believe in Heaven, Hell or anything else. I know what I believe in and it isn't that. "Mum, you have to calm down."

"Who are you?"

"It's me. Your son, Christopher."

Patty has figured it out as well by now. "Little Chris?"

I nod. "I don't know exactly what's going on, but I'm going to get you out. Get us *all* out."

"They've done such terrible things to people," Patty tells her daughter.

"I still don't understand."

We aren't allowed any more time to figure things out, because once again the door opens and the robed men march in. Three this time. They might be coming to take Dixon away, or do something to Patty—Gran—but I don't want to find out which. Already the cameras are appearing, descending to film events.

"Stay away from them!" I shout. "I'm not kidding."

They ignore me. One points to Dixon, then turns in the direction of Patty's cage. The final figure stands between me and my Mum.

It all happens in a flash, but like all moments of intensity, it also slows right down to a crawl. Out of the corner of my eye I see Dixon rise; he's only been pretending to be dead. Through the bars he grabs hold of the closest guard and reaches into his cloak. There's a sudden bang as Dixon shoots the guy. Too late the chains holding the old man begin to tighten.

Another shot, and the monk nearest to me catches a bullet in the arm. He staggers close enough to my cage I can drag him into the bars, knocking him out cold. Quickly, before my own chains haul me back, I fumble inside his robes and pull out the keys they always use. My shackles are beginning to pull tight, so I see to them first—both feet. Then one hand... I only have time for the one, before I have to make a start on the cage lock. I'm being dragged backwards by one arm. I stretch to try and turn the key a final time.

A third shot, and Dixon is dead—really dead, this time. The only monk left has seen to that. I'm still struggling with the key, but manage to turn it, unlocking the cage.

The door flies open.

Is it my imagination, or are the other two cages growing smaller? Compressing? Gran and Mum hold up their hands as the bars shrink. I look up and the same is true of my own cage. They're trying to crush us.

Gran is the first to feel the full force of it, when the bars come down on her head. She shrieks as the metal grinds up her old bones, the cracks like... footsteps on brittle twigs. Mum's faring about the same, her body surrendering to the cage that is mashing her frame.

I have one last lock to undo, holding my left wrist.

Don't drop it, don't drop it. You can still save them.

But I know, even as I undo the clasp, jumping out of my cage just as it collapses in on itself, it's already too late for Gran and Mum. They've become so much blood, bone and metal: a fusion of human and cage.

The monk nearest my gran turns the gun he used to kill Dixon on me. Gritting my teeth, I run at him, hitting him squarely in the stomach with my head and winding him before he can get off a shot. "You bastard! You fucking bastard! You killed them!" If I'd been thinking rationally, I'd have realised that Gran—at least—had been dead long before she turned up here as 'Patty'.

I rip off his hood, pulling the material back to reveal a bald-headed face. The strange thing is the monk's blindfolded, just as I had been when I was first brought here. Someone has drilled a hole in the centre of his forehead.

The sight of this only gives me pause for a moment, before I smash that face in. Pummelling it into the floor with my fist, the anger welling up inside me.

When there's hardly anything left of the head, I stop, breathing hard. I'm aware of something hovering over me, several somethings in fact: the cameras.

I grab the pistol from the dead monk and point it at one of

them.

Before I can pull the trigger, the door to the right of me opens.

I look from the spherical camera, to my escape route. What's this, some kind of reward? A piece of cheese at the end of the maze?

Don't know, don't care. Trying to keep my eyes fixed ahead of me, and off my mangled relatives, I head out through the door.

To freedom!

Interlude: Three Days Ago

I evaded them for about a day and a half, but only because I knew this area so well.

In the end, there was nowhere left to hide. Where can you hide from something that's all around you, that can see you even though you can't see them? They directed the men to me, just as they'd sent Kim to the shack.

I was in the jungle where giant snakes and lions lived, and down by the water there were man-eating crocodiles.

There were quite a few of them, probably trained in tracking, ex-military—I caught a glimpse of a pair of boots in the undergrowth at one point, before waiting for whoever it was to go by. These weren't any police I was familiar with; no doctors either. They'd told Kim what she wanted to hear, just like those adverts did to the poor unfortunates who bought the stuff they peddled.

They wanted to find me, and silence me.

Because if the secret ever got out, it would be the end of everything. Humanity would never be the same again.

They watch and wait, They watch and wait... It went through my head over and over, trains on a track. It's what I'd written on the pages Kim had read, apparently. Or was it just what we were allowed to see?

Piloting my spaceship into the deeper reaches of the Galaxy, battling one-eyed aliens with veiny skins.

Maybe things change when you try to set them down: hints were one thing, in books, on TV, in movies. But the cold, hard truth—facts unearthing how far this all goes back—that was another.

Oblivious as we were, we'd created ways of letting the knowledge creep out into the world, whether it was through cave paintings, ancient mythology or even posters (and then They'd tampered with the results). It was a chicken and egg situation: without Them, there would have been no human evolution, and without human evolution would They be able to survive?

Symbiosis? Hardly. How could any one-sided relationship be called that? We were subordinates. Blind and obedient, given the illusion of free will when all the time we were being herded towards our own doom.

"Ah, but if you push us too far, if we destroy ourselves, what will you do then—eh?" Without thinking, I had asked the question out loud. And that was my final mistake.

Something rustled nearby; they'd heard me and were on my trail. I ran, just as I had that day when I was young. I misplaced my footing and suddenly I was falling, head over heels, down an incline. Something thudded into my side, silent and deadly. It might have been a branch; more likely it was a dart from a tranquiliser gun.

I was already beginning to feel its effects, growing woozy as I reached the bottom. My vision was blurring, I was passing out.

They'd hunted me like the animal I was (to them, or more accurately their superiors). When I woke, who knew where I would be.

Or if I would remember any of this until it was too late.

Seven

I make my way down a darkened corridor, pistol in my hand.

One of the cameras is following me over my shoulder. I can sense it there, just far enough behind to stay out of my way, but near enough to film my escape.

There are other doors down the corridor. I stop to kick the first one in, thinking maybe I can save some prisoners. Inside, there are more Pain Cages, those round hanging jails, each containing a body. A human being.

Seven in here. I don't recognise any of the faces… No, wait, that's not true. Malone is here. I think I used to work for him at one point. Yeah, that's right. Malone! I told him where to get off for some reason.

"Christopher, help me," he pleads, sticking his hand through the bars. "They're trying to kill us all."

"I know," I tell him. "Hold on."

"Chris! Chris! Please…" The voice comes from behind me, muffled and odd, from another room opposite. That's one I do know; very well. "Dad?"

I rush out, back into the corridor, ignoring the cries from Malone. I kick open the other door, only to see my father in one of the pain cages. His head is encased in a see-through glass case. Brown liquid is pouring in from above, fast, and he is only just keeping his head above its level.

"Always… always said the drink would… would get me," he spits.

I take aim with the gun, but I'm not a sure enough shot. I could very easily hit Dad. I rush to the cage, shaking it, wishing I'd kept the keys that had freed me—though there was nothing to say they'd fit the locks in here.

The liquid covers his mouth and nose. Dad smiles, then panics, begins to jerk. I'm watching a dead man drown right before my eyes.

"No, no." I close my eyes. "You're *making* me see this. You've still got me whacked up on drugs or something. I know now. I understand."

"You understand nothing," says a woman's voice from behind me. I turn, seeing Kim in another one of the cages. She's naked, but also shackled, chained at the waist as well as the hands and feet.

"No… Not you, as well," I moan.

A huge spike is rising from the bottom of the cage, up and up. "Mmmm… Oh yes," she says, licking her lips. Then she impales herself on the spike, leaping back gladly onto it. I wince as she jumps up and down on the sharp skewer, blood gushing from between her legs. "Take me… Take me beyond my limits! Harder! Oh God, harder! Hurt me, hurt me!" One last impalement and the spike comes up and out of her mouth accompanied by a fountain of redness.

"Kim! No…" She hangs lifeless on the spike, arms limp as the chains loosen. There are more of the cameras in the room, lenses focused on Dad and Kim. "Are you getting all of this, you sick motherfuckers!"

Unsurprisingly, there is no answer.

I dash back out, feeling like I'm going to throw up. What the fuck is going on? It sounds insane, but my mind offers yet another explanation: maybe whoever was responsible for all this could just pluck people out of time—living or dead—for their own personal amusement. Is that it? Is that the explanation?

Kicking in door after door, I see people in the throes of agony, being tortured, being killed in so many different ways that they all blur into one eventually. But I can't help any of them.

I pelt down the corridor, figuring that if I can get to the outside world I might just be able to bring back help. The corridor stretches away from me, though, Vertigo-style. The walls, floor and tunnel ahead are melting. To be replaced by

A landscape. A panoramic view of pain.

Pain cages: hundreds, thousands, possibly millions of them. Too many to count. The screams and wails are deafening; a torture in itself.

I drop the pistol—it falls away into nothingness—and clasp my hands to my ears. As I blink, focussing on each cage in turn, I see faces that I know (like my Uncle and Kim's parents), many that I don't, but I also see objects: toys I used to play with as a child; the ghost story book I was given as a prize at school for writing essays in class; the first jacket I ever bought for myself, a leather one I thought looked so cool; my old computer; sweet and sour chicken, my favourite meal… There are places as well, locations: behind the bike sheds where I first touched a girl's breast; the local cinema that had been replaced by a multiplex; the call centre; the flat where Kim and I shared so many moments…

All of these are inside pain cages of their own, being torn apart, destroyed in various ways. It is then and only then that I truly get what's happening.

The cages form a ring, and in the centre of this is an open space—like a gladiatorial arena. I take away my hands, to find that a silence had descended more deafening than any screams. Several of the round cameras zip past me and into the arena, and I follow their trail with my eyes. Down to a table surrounded by men.

A rhythmic beeping starts up, then continues. *Beep-Beep-Beep…* The sound of a heartbeat. I see now that it's coming from a monitor on the side. At first I assume the men are dressed in robes like the monks, but then I see my error. Their surgical gowns swish when they walk, in much the same way.

Their mouths are covered by masks, but then so are their eyes. Again, blindfolded, the round headpieces that they wear, the circular mirror reflectors, are the only eyes they appear to have.

They shouldn't even be operating, but they are. They're cutting into a man's skull, taking chunks of it away and… exposing the brain.

"Now we have to excise the damaged tissue. Good God, how many brain cells has it affected?"

Cells… Brain cells. Pain cells… Pain cages! The link becomes clear, even though I'm finding it harder and harder to concentrate. For one thing I only have to look at the cages themselves, which are becoming more like liquid, the surrounding area red and meaty, like an organic city I once saw.

"Look at the size of that tumour. If only we'd got to it before."

Steps have appeared leading downwards, and I descend to observe the operation. The doctors murmur to one another, conferring. The circular cameras—the globes—are capturing each second of it. As infected brain tissue, infected memories, are cut away. People's faces, those familiar and those only glimpsed for a second… A writer's imagination providing the character backgrounds and personalities of those it couldn't possibly know. An obnoxious estate agent who once showed me round a house, a fitness instructor bumped into just the once during a brief visit to the gym, a man I once saw preaching religion on the streets… These and many more besides.

And I recognise the face of the guy on the table—how could I not?

The man lying there has his father's chin, his mother's eyes.

I want to tell them to stop, but I know they won't hear me.

Then I'm asleep again.

But one day… Yes, one day I will wake.

Epilogue

Am I awake or still asleep?

It's hard to tell the difference anymore. I'm in a cage… no, a cell. It's white, the walls are soft, spongy. I'm shackled by my hands and my feet. They tell me I'm dangerous, the doctors: a danger to myself and to others. I hurt some people once upon a time, then again in here. I don't remember any of it.

I'm not sure who the woman is who comes to visit me every so often. She says her name is Kim, but I don't remember her. I remember the very first time she came, though, the conversation she had with Dr Banberry, who was in charge of my case back then. I lay in bed recuperating, the air tickling my bald scalp, my stitches itching.

"Can he hear what we're saying?" she asked him.

"We're not sure. Possibly. It's a side effect of the operation, I'm afraid. He may stay like this forever, or… The damage the tumour did was quite severe, so it's best not to get your hopes up. It definitely affected the TPRV1 receptors in the brain. Oh, I'm sorry, the transient receptor potential vanilloid subtype. Pain receptors in layman's terms. But these have also recently been linked in studies to memory and learning. If he does come out of this state, then it's likely he won't remember much."

"And that was also the cause of his… delusions? The tumour?"

Banberry looked at her seriously. "Undoubtedly. That mixed with the drugs and drink he was taking at the time of his disappearance. We call it altered perception. A warped view of reality that feels completely real to the person suffering its effects. Other symptoms include seeing things that aren't really there, memory lapses"

"Like when he rang me and couldn't remember doing it."

"Exactly."

No, no. I didn't have a phone! I didn't! My mind conjured up the words, but I had no idea what they meant. That particular recollection was gone.

There were tears in the woman's eyes, as she looked from me to Banberry. "How did this happen? I don't understand."

"Could have been something that happened a few years ago. Could have been a knock on the head when he was a kid, just waiting for a trigger. Who knows?"

A monster… running from a monster. Dixon! Who's Dixon? No, no. I banged my head after I saw what he had written. Didn't I? What are you talking about? Who. The Fuck. Is Dixon?

"There's no point speculating about it, no point beating yourself up."

"But I saw he was acting strangely, obsessive, not like the old Christopher. I should have done something then. Instead I just left him."

"You weren't to know." Banberry comforted her by patting her arm; all he could muster.

When the woman called Kim looked at me again, I felt a trickle of dribble running from the corner of my mouth.

It's good of her to keep coming back, I suppose. To keep talking to me like I'm normal. But I know I'm not. When I'm asleep— or awake? dreaming, yes, dreaming—I sometimes imagine that this was done to me on purpose. That I found out something so terrifying I had to be silenced.

Like the fact that there's something out there, making human beings inflict pain on each other because it feeds off it. Yes, that's right. That's

I can only hold on to the notion for a short time then it drifts away from me.

But I *do* remember the cages. I saw them a long time ago.

They had something to do with pain. Some kind of connection I can't grasp now no matter how hard I try.

I think once I had a story to tell about them. About how we're all inside these cages, in one form or another, but don't really know it. About things with one eyes that watch and wait.

What They're waiting for, I have no idea—I don't think I'll ever find out.

All I know is that They really do understand the nature of pain, true pain.

Just as I, myself, once did.

Secrets

I could tell as soon as he walked through the door that he wasn't your average frequenter of Mick's place.

For a start he wore a suit. Sure, it was tatty and scuffed at the sleeves, but it was a suit all the same. And his black shoes looked like they'd been shiny at one time or another.

But the man himself, well that was a different matter. Deathly pale skin was stretched tight over his face—especially at the cheekbones, which threatened to break through at any moment—and what little hair he had on his head was slicked back; plastered to his dome-shaped scalp.

And those eyes! I swear when he looked round the room you could feel the shivers going down the spines of the regulars... those who were still sober at that time of night, anyway. Then his intense gaze settled on me at the bar. I felt him drilling into my head with those piercing blue orbs, wielded with all the skill of a trained hypnotist. I tried to look away, but found myself losing this battle of wills.

In the end it was the man who broke off the connection. He approached the bar—quick strides at first then slowing as he reached his destination. Placing a bony hand on the counter, he leaned on this for support. I remember thinking he'd probably fall down if that makeshift crutch was removed, like that guy in that famous clip from a certain sit-com they always showed.

Shirl, over at the far end, kept her distance. She had no intentions of coming near, let alone serving this guy. I couldn't say I really blamed her. Yet something about him fascinated me, don't ask what or why. Finally, I plucked up the courage to speak.

"What'll it be?" I asked quietly.

He looked at me and replied in a strong, deep voice that betrayed no hint of a discernible accent, "Scotch. Bring it over to the corner booth." With that he left a crumpled bill on the bar and shambled over to the table.

My palms were sweating as I fixed his drink. When he slid onto the green leather bench, I heard his bones crack like shots from a rifle. He stared at me again as I brought the scotch over. "There you go. Is that all you want?"

He nodded, groaning with the effort.

"Okay, well enjoy your drink then." I was just about to turn when he grabbed my arm. I was so startled, I nearly dropped my tray.

"Sit down," he whispered.

"Really, I can't. I'm working and—"

"Sit down." There was no threat in his invitation and the grip wasn't particularly strong—with those frail hands how could it be?—but I obeyed all the same. Maybe it was those eyes, maybe he was a hypnotist of some kind, I thought. The bar was pretty slow that Thursday, however, and Shirl could handle any customers that might drift in. I figured, what's the harm?

He still had hold of my wrist, and I could feel him fingering the skin for a pulse. The man closed his eyes a fraction, still looking at me but through the slits. Then a chilling smile swept across his face and he let go.

"You are someone with a great deal on his mind," he said simply.

I frowned. "How do you—?"

"I am very perceptive. Perhaps you would like to tell me about your wife and child."

I hesitated, the words throwing me completely. Most people had things on their mind, that could have been pure guesswork. But not this. Somehow he *knew*. I still said, "I-I don't know what you're talking about."

"Yes you do. They left you, didn't they?"

"How could you...?" It wasn't possible for him to know these things, unless... "Did Hannah send you? Where is she? *Please*, I need to know."

"Calm yourself," he said. "I have never met your wife. I am merely an... interested party."

"A lawyer?" I was angry, yet something was keeping me in check.

"No. I am here to help you."

I don't know why—maybe it was a quality in this guy's voice—but I believed him. When he asked me again to unburden myself, I instantly complied. "I haven't a clue how it got so out of hand. We were fine, y'know? Everything was great until… well, I screwed things up basically. I thought I'd got it under control, the gambling. I kept telling myself one more bet and I'd get my lucky break."

He laughed out loud at this remark, as if he knew something I didn't. Several of the regulars jerked awake and looked over. The man waited for them to turn away before saying: "Continue."

"I got myself into a bit of a mess. I'm just about hanging on to this job but have no idea how I'm going to… When Hannah found out, she went crazy. We'd already been having problems, and I guess this topped it off. She left last Saturday, taking Danny with her. I haven't heard from them since."

The Stranger leant forward. "So tell me, what do you desire most in the world?"

"What?" His question came out of nowhere, and again I was caught off guard.

"I asked what you would like most in the world."

I had a feeling he already knew—he seemed to know everything else—plus it was pretty obvious from my sob story, but I told him anyway. "Okay, I want a chance to prove I can change. Make a fresh start. I'd do anything to get them back."

His smile was twisted. "Good, good. What if I told you there was a way to do that? That I could arrange it?"

It was my turn to laugh. This was ridiculous, how could such a bizarre excuse of a man possibly fix my life? All the same, curiosity got the better of me and I heard him out.

"I know what you are thinking, but I can help you." He paused here for effect more than anything. "I ask only that you help me in return," he added.

There was an authority in his tone, the patter of a master manipulator or con artist, but for once in my life I dared to hope. "What can I do?"

He gulped the scotch greedily; a trickle broke free and ran

down his chin. Then he steepled his fingers and began. "What I am about to tell you is a secret only a handful of people have ever known. Of that handful, only two retained their sanity once they were 'enlightened'. Shall I go on?"

I nodded vaguely, not really grasping what he meant.

"Then understand this. I am not what I appear to be."

His story was a crazy one, a joke told with the straightest of faces. I sat there as he informed me that we are not in control of our own destinies; that there are beings who exist on a plane to the left of our world. Watching us, keeping records, regulating mankind from behind the scenes. And he, this strange man who sat opposite me, had been one of the clan.

"It has happened before," he said quietly. "Members of our race have spoken out about the intense misery we have caused your people. Wars, disease, prejudice… all were our doing. They were the few who developed a conscience over time. They grew weary of deciding who lived, who died, who succeeded and who failed. But they were quickly silenced. Only one or two dared breach the barrier and escape."

"Where to?"

"Here, of course." He looked around the bar, over my shoulder, before continuing. "Some went to ground and have never been heard of since, living in hiding, in secret. Others were not so fortunate."

At first I thought this man was quite clearly insane. But he had one hell of an imagination, I'd give him that. And the more I listened, the more I began to get drawn into his fantasy. Again, I wondered if it was his eyes, because he hardly took them off me throughout his little performance. Anyway, I decided to play along with him for the time being.

"So what do you want from me?" I asked.

He smiled that terrifying, all-knowing smile once more. The grin of a teacher who has all the answers to a particularly hard exam. "It will become clear in time, but first we must go. Leave this place. It is far from safe."

He obviously believed what he was saying, but the rational side of my brain was finally waking up. After that, my patience wore thin pretty quickly. "I'm not going anywhere. Look, I've listened to what you had to say—and frankly it's not my help you need, it's—"

"I know it is hard, but what I have told you is the truth. You *have* to believe me," he pleaded.

"I'm sorry, I've got a bar to run… while they still let me."

The man sighed and bowed his head as I got up and walked away from the table. I'd barely taken three steps when the lights above blinked on and off. Now, we've had plenty of surges before at Mick's, but this was something else. The fluorescent panels were winking in a uniform way, almost as if they were tapping out a message in Morse Code. The remaining customers reared their heads, as did Shirl—who hadn't moved from the other end of the bar.

I turned to look at my mysterious acquaintance in the booth. His head was still bowed, and I could see a bead of sweat trailing down his temple. He only said four words, but they were enough: "I have been found."

I rushed back to join him, and when I touched his shoulder the man jumped. He stared up at me, eyes wide with panic—blood vessels throbbing in the corners. I recognised that look, I'd seen it in the mirror when people were after me for money I owed them. "Come on," I said. "There's a back door to this place."

I don't know what made me help, I hadn't really changed my mind about his story: his tale of omnipotent creatures who played with us like dolls in a Wendy House. Or the deal he'd talked about if I went with him. But the man was obviously terrified of somebody, or something. I couldn't just stand idly by, even if he was a crackpot.

We stumbled out into the alley behind Mick's. My new friend could barely walk, so I had to half carry him past the trash cans and litter. "I'll get you into a taxi. You can find your own way from there," I grunted as we shuffled along.

It was fairly dark, the only light coming from the windows in the buildings above, and as we made our way down that passage I suddenly became very nervous. The street was about fifty, maybe sixty metres away, but it might as well have been a thousand. The man was much heavier than he looked and the further we got, the slower we went. His feet scraped noisily on the floor with each step I took.

Then I heard a noise behind me, a kind of sizzle like frying bacon—only much louder. I turned, but wished to God I'd just kept going.

The sight froze me up, all thoughts of getting away vanished. The passageway was losing its coherence, the walls and floor melting into a kind of slop. It whirled around clockwise to form an ellipse, an opening of some sort.

As I stood there dumbstruck, several figures emerged. It was hard to make out exact details because of the haze around the 'door'—this *back* door to our world it seemed—but they appeared to be wearing hooded cloaks.

There was no time to run, they were all around us in an instant. Had formed a circle around us, in fact. Up close, I could see that those were no cloaks—but rather a thick, leathery membrane that hid their bodies and faces. A mesmerising blue light shone from under those 'hoods'.

One reached out a hand: a gnarled, twisted and revolting limb, yet it clamped on to the man's shoulder with all the power of a robot on an assembly line. Another slipped its arm around his throat.

Though I was shaking, and about two seconds away from throwing up, I tried to get between these things and the Stranger. There was a sudden explosion of light and stars, and suddenly I was bent double on the ground, feeling pain like I'd never felt before.

Another one of the creatures stood over me. He seemed huge at the time, but couldn't have been much taller than me. I gaped up through watery eyes as he peeled back that fleshy cowl.

There was no mouth or nose that I could see and its skin was transparent, with tiny bones and raised veins patterning its face. Its cheeks bulged, like the Stranger's, and the lack of hair betrayed a distinct family resemblance. It scrutinised me with its single cobalt eye, planted in the middle of its 'face'. There wasn't a sliver of white in that eye, and it felt like the stunning blue orb was going to set me alight.

"No!" cried the man to my right, dropping the façade of humanity. I had no idea how he was speaking because now he didn't have a mouth either, but it was his voice I could hear. "You cannot!"

It glared at him with contempt, then faced me once more. Just when I thought the death blow would be dealt, it walked off to join its brethren. The first pair picked the Stranger up by the arms—he was still in the process of changing at that point, two eyes merging to become the one, his coat lengthening, gaining a hood, wrapping itself around him—and they marched him back to the shrinking hole in time and space. I couldn't move, let alone shout out for help. Not that it would have done any good.

And, as they disappeared, the weird smog trailing in their wake, I heard the man's distinctive voice one final time. "My promise is fulfilled."

I must have passed out then, because all I remember is blackness.

*

It wasn't until a day or so later that I found out what he meant. Hannah and Danny showed up unexpectedly at the flat; she wanted to give our marriage another try. I should have been thrilled, it was what I'd wished for. A fresh start.

But the events of that night, which I can't share with anyone, least of all my family, have left a stain on my soul. The secrets he shared… the knowledge that this is all pointless, that whatever decision, whatever choice we make is preordained, programmed into our minds at every step, is enough to make the sanest person lose it completely.

Now I know *They* exist, I can think of nothing else. And what used to be a happy life—for the most part—now seems so hollow. The only thing keeping me from going off the rails is the fact that I might somehow be different. If I wasn't, then they would have finished me off back in that alley behind Mick's. Maybe I can't be directed as easily as my wife and kid.

Perhaps that will be the key to their downfall?

But what about the fugitive from their world? I have no idea what happened to him, what punishment they meted out for his disloyalty. I sometimes watch for his return at night, though (I don't sleep so well these days) hoping he'll come back and tell me what he wanted me to do, why he chose me. I guess in my heart of hearts I know that will never happen.

All I do know is, one day there will have to be a reckoning—when more and more people find out about these 'Controllers'. And maybe on that day the human race will be granted its freedom.

Until then, I can only watch...

And wait.

The Scoop

Adam Regis always felt like his life was out of control, but he really didn't know the half of it.

To some extent, he'd always known that the job, the situation he'd found himself in, wasn't a choice. He'd sit and listen in awe to his Uncle Steve when he came to visit, soaking up the tales of criminals he was writing about, of murders, of chats with film and TV stars—he was always at some premiere or another. It was almost inevitable that Adam would want to follow in his footsteps rather than be a teacher like his own dad. He saw enough of those at school, and hated most of them. Why on earth would he ever want to become one?

'Course, as people get older they realise that things aren't really as black and white (ha!) as all that. Teaching was a noble profession, and if he'd spent more time listening to what they were trying to tell him maybe he wouldn't have ended up in such a mess.

Then again…

Still, wasn't as exciting or glamorous as the life of a reporter, was it? No, nothing beat the glamour of chasing stories about a local pub that was being turned into an apartment block, or plans for a new bypass, or even that old faithful: a cat being rescued from a tree by plucky firemen. Believe it or not—and Adam didn't—those were some of his first gigs on *The Herald*, the very paper his uncle had worked for. The life of a jobbing reporter. And it wasn't long after he'd got back from his first few assignments that Adam realised good old Stevie had been, not to put too fine a point on it, full of shit. Should have gone into fiction; the man was certainly good at making things up!

Steve had, though, also gone missing in mysterious circumstances, never to be seen ever again—something else that led to Adam taking up his mantle when he was old enough to do so. Hadn't been that difficult, either; the editor remembered his uncle, remembered the name. "Damned fine reporter, Steve," the man had said, shaking his head. "Damned fine. If you end up being half the word jockey he was, we'll be doing all right."

Well, Adam liked to think that in all these years he'd ended up being better. He'd studied everything he could find written by his uncle, discovered that the nearest he'd come to criminals and gangsters had been attending a few fraud trials, and the nearest to stars had been if he covered the horoscopes when old Peg was on her holidays. Always searching for that elusive headline, that big news hook. Sadly, it had taken his disappearance for Steve Regis to get anywhere near a huge story, and even then he had been the subject of it; at the centre of various conspiracy theories that had taken on a life of their own over time. Adam didn't intend to wait around for something like that to make his name.

Maybe it had been the mundanity of the tasks he kept getting given, or maybe it had been digging into what had really happened to his uncle (coming up empty every time), but in his free time Adam began to investigate more interesting topics. Other disappearances... or abductions, as he discovered. Some of the people had been returned and claimed that aliens snatched them; others that creatures from the sea had been responsible; still others that ghosts had whisked them away to the other side. It all fed into his obsession with the outlandish, the macabre and the supernatural that he'd had in his teenage years—which probably stemmed from those Herbert Lynch horror novels Steve used to bring him whenever he visited. Made him more willing to listen, to believe. Gave him the drive to find out about the unknown, the big mysteries. To solve them if he could...

Once the rest of the office caught wind of this, of course, he got called things like 'Kolchak' (which he'd had to look up) and 'Mulder' (more recent). He was also given all the crackpot stories to follow up that nobody wanted. Looking into markings that had started cropping up on trees in a nearby woods... that was just kids mucking about, carving nonsense into the trunks. Getting to the bottom of why the river that ran through the park was turning red... that was down to a butcher dumping his offcuts further upstream. He even had to go and investigate a spate of pet disappearances—dogs, cats, even a rabbit from someone's garden in one instance—which had turned out to be nothing more than a couple of guys stealing them and flogging the animals at car boot sales.

Adam had carried on with his more 'serious' enquiries at the same time, however. "You wait, one of these cases is going to lead to the nationals," he'd tell his colleagues, who'd just snigger and make jokes. But Adam was also thinking perhaps a book, TV appearances. If he played this right, who knew where it would lead?

He looked into all sorts, from various methods of fortune-telling and psychic readings to angel sightings and spiritual healing; from poltergeists and reports of possession to theories about mutants and genetic disorders. As with the day job, many turned out to be fake or just led nowhere, but every now and again he'd stumble onto something worth his time and effort.

Like the fellow he'd come across while looking into near-death experiences, OBEs and astral projection. That had been what kicked everything off really, his story—which Adam had a devil of a job getting out of him. This was in spite of the fact he was in a nursing home now and said he was grateful of the company, the chance to chat to *anyone*. The man had soon clammed up when he found out the real reason for Adam's visit, though. More than that, he seemed scared.

"Mr Sutton, I can understand your reluctance to talk about all this—but believe me, I won't judge and I won't laugh."

The old man had stared at Adam gravely. "Laugh? I don't expect you to *laugh* at all. There's nothing to laugh about in all this."

Adam had been even more intrigued when he heard this, and pressed his subject for information.

"What I know, what I saw, could change the world, lad. It's not something that... I shouldn't be talking about this, I really shouldn't."

"*Please*," Adam had said, leaning forward in his chair.

Mr Sutton cocked his head. "Well, I suppose if you've found me, it's only because *They* wanted you to."

"Who?"

And then he told him, the whole story—nothing held back. About what he'd seen once when using his astral projection talents. It was the most outrageous and unbelievable thing Adam had ever heard, and that was saying something; yet he did not judge, did not laugh. Did not feel like laughing at all.

It was clear from the way he told his tale, from his reluctance to tell it in the first place, that Mr Sutton thought it was all real. But even if he could project himself into that other place—the *real* other side—where They resided, that wasn't to say that his mind hadn't been playing tricks on him.

Nevertheless, Adam left that day with his recordings—with Mr Sutton's apologies for ruining his life ringing in his ears—and with a newfound need, no, *urgent* desire, to find out everything he could about these... these Controllers, as the old man had called them. To track down more of the people that might have been affected by them; though, if it was all true, then that included every single person on the planet. But there were others out there who knew about all this, who'd had direct contact perhaps. Adam was certain of it.

What's more, he was determined to find them.

From that day onwards, this new project eclipsed all the others. It would make a book on its own, he reasoned, maybe even several volumes. At the very least a series of articles that would rival those about the Mothmen or the Slender Man phenomenon.

His research led him to a woman named Kim Munro (nee Burke), whose former partner Chris had talked about—even written about—one-eyed creatures who controlled mankind.

"I... I feel terrible about it all," said the woman as she brought Adam a cup of tea and sat opposite him in her living room. Adam had told her he was writing a medical paper about what happened, otherwise she probably wouldn't have let him through the door. "Should have realised there was something terribly wrong with him earlier. Maybe then..." There were tears welling in her eyes even now, thinking about it.

"The tumour," Adam stated and she nodded.

"Made him act so strangely. Forget things, become obsessed

with other things. And… well, he could be violent at times," she told him, looking down at the floor. "It changed his whole personality."

"Do you have any of his writings at all?" Adam asked her, more to change the subject than anything. "Something that shows the state of mind he was in during his decline?"

"I… wait here a minute," said the woman and left him alone for a short while. Adam looked around at the photos in the room; of Kim with another man, a wedding picture; others of a couple of kids. She'd moved on from what had happened—yet hadn't really, that much was obvious.

"Here we go," she said on her return, causing him to start. "Oh, I'm sorry, I didn't mean to…" Kim handed him a folder and he opened it up. Inside were stories, double-spaced; Adam scanned the first pages of a couple. They were actually pretty good, and chillingly close to what Mr Sutton had told him. As fantastic as it sounded, was it possible that the tumour had been allowing Chris access to these creatures without him knowing it? At the bottom were other papers, little more than rough drawings. A blue ellipsis: the eye. He pulled one of these out and held it up, letters scrawled on it as if a child had written them.

"What does this mean?"

Kim reached over, took the paper and looked at it. "It was what he'd been writing when I found him. When he phoned me to say where he was, just before…"

Adam read the words again when she handed it back. 'They watch and wait.'

He must have been frowning because she added: "It had something to do with those stories, with what he was telling me at the end. He was talking about Nostradamus and gods who need us to be damaged and… It's hard to remember exactly, he was in a bit of a state—and so was I, frankly. He'd been looking for patterns in it all, he said. Art, literature, in the world around us. Everything was scrambled up inside his brain."

Or maybe he was just seeing things more clearly than most, thought Adam.

Kim still visited the man, when she got the chance, but her

new husband didn't really know much about Chris. She felt it was better that way. But she told Adam where to find him, and he'd gone along to visit at the hospital.

What he'd found was a fellow locked away in a room, with only the barest of home comforts. His hair was cut short and the scar on his scalp was still visible from the lengthy operation he'd endured. The man was simply staring out through the grilled window, though it wasn't clear what he was looking at; certainly not the view, which was of a concrete wall. Maybe he wasn't seeing what was out there anyway, Adam mused.

"Good luck!" the muscular nurse had said when he let him in, Adam having told him he was a relative. He approached the man cautiously, given what his ex had said about violence, but he needn't have worried. The Chris Warwick sitting here wasn't the Chris Warwick she had known before, or even something that resembled a human being. Spittle ran from one corner of his mouth and when Adam called his name Chris was barely responsive. He even waved a hand in front of his face, but there was no blinking; nothing.

It wasn't until Adam pulled out the drawing of the blue ellipse, not until he spoke the words from the other piece of paper that he got a response—though even then it was only a twitch of the cheek muscle.

"They watch and wait, Chris. What did you mean by that? You have to try and remember."

The man whispered something then, a bubble of saliva popping on his lips as he did so.

"What? What was that?" asked Adam, leaning in.

The man repeated what he'd said, grunting it this time. "S-S-Sellsss…"

"Cells?" asked the reporter. "What—"

"K-K-Kajjjjjus…" Then one word that was as clear as day: "Pain!"

Then he leaned back, the effort having clearly exhausted him. Adam got nothing more from him that afternoon—nor during the other times he'd visited, the man obviously little more than a vegetable.

But he'd thought a lot about what he'd been trying to say. Was he talking about his room being a cell, a cage? Was he *in* pain? Adam hugely doubted that, not with the amount of meds he was on. Even if he'd been clear-headed, Chris would have had a hard time concentrating on anything.

Or was he talking about that eye? The... what, ghosts, spirits Mr Sutton had claimed he'd seen inside it? The prisoners?

His investigations began to take over his life. They definitely got in the way of him having any kind of a relationship, not that he'd been any great shakes in that department in the first place. Even if he was of a mind to seek out a one-night stand, he wouldn't be able to invite them back to his bed-sit because he'd turned one of the walls into an evidence board, with bits of paper stuck to it, maps and pins with thread connecting the dots. A picture building up... a pattern.

It got in the way of seeing family and what few friends he had; now the story was all-consuming. Now he really couldn't stop, even if he wanted to—and Adam began to wonder how much of that was down to him at all? Maybe, if those things were real, they wanted him to tell their story? Didn't seem very likely, but...

Adam's next port of call was to follow up a set of rumours. The drunken ramblings of a guy who kept starting fights and getting thrown out of bars. Didn't take long to find him, and by the time Adam did the man had already been at the booze. Another couple and he was ready to tell his secrets, once they'd moved into one of the more private booths.

"Sshh!" said the guy, pressing his index finger against his lips. "I'm not supposed to be talking about all this." He'd been slurring his words even before Adam came along, and the drinks he'd bought him had done little to help with his enunciation. Not to mention his attention span. "Used to work in a place just like this, y'know?" he told Adam with a hiccup.

"Right," the reporter said, humouring him. "If we could just get back to the—"

"Mick's!" shouted the man, so loudly that some of the other patrons of the place turned and looked over at them.

"Right," Adam said again.

"That's where… Hey, it was in a booth just like this one. That's where it started." One of his eyes was practically a slit, the other red-raw, and he was jabbing that same index finger at Adam. "That's where it… it ended as well."

"Where what ended?"

"No, no, no, no. *No!*" the man said then. "Not in the booth. I-I didn't believe him, y'see? Not… not right away. Even though he… Well, he *knew* things. Knew my family had walked out."

"Who did?"

The man flapped his hand, as if trying to remember something. Perhaps his train of thought? "The… He wasn't who he… What he looked like. He was in disguise." The guy winked then conspiratorially.

Adam sighed. This was getting them nowhere. "I'm trying to find out what you know about…" He looked about him. "About *Them.*"

"Who?"

"You know who I'm talking about; you've been heard shooting your mouth off."

"I… I haven't said anything." He looked worried now. Scared even, like Mr Sutton had done. Then he lowered his voice. "Haven't said anything that *wasn't true*, friend."

"You've seen them, haven't you?"

He didn't answer for a moment, then suddenly shouted: "Another round! Barmaid! Over here, another round on my new drinking buddy!"

Adam nodded. If that was what it took to get answers out of him, then so be it. What answers the guy might be able to manage by the time he was finished was another matter, though. He looked for a moment like he was going to be sick, then just belched. His breath reeked.

The barmaid brought over more drinks and Adam thanked her.

"Yeah, thanks Shirl." The woman looked at him, confused, then just shook her head.

"This… this person you were talking about," Adam prompted once she was out of earshot again. "The one in disguise."

"Fixed things for me!" said the man, knocking back his drink in one. "He fixed them real good."

"I don't understand."

"Quid... pro... quo..." He said each word slowly, as if it was Adam who was having a hard time understanding. "I helped him. Well, I *tried*. Tried to get him away, but..." The man shook his head, then looked like he was regretting it, swaying a little in the booth.

"Hey... Hey!" It was Adam's turn to shout now, reaching out and grabbing his shoulder, more to steady him than anything. "Don't you pass out on me."

"No... No, I..." He paused again, then said suddenly: "That's when I saw those things. When I was tryin' to... To help him. To help him escape. But there's no real escape from Them. I realise that now. I used to think I was different. That I was... That they couldn't..." His sentence got away from him again, so he began another. "He was one of them, you know. He did escape once."

"This person you helped?" Adam asked, checking his phone to make sure he was still recording the conversation.

The man nodded. "Was living in... what do you call it?"

"Hiding?"

"In... incognito! Wasn't the only one, either. Said there were others. Said other people knew as well." He looked down. "My glass is empty."

Adam waved for more drinks, and when the man had knocked back another large scotch, he continued: "But they got him. Took him back with them. I thought he was the one who'd fixed it all, gave them back to me."

"Your family?"

There were tears in the man's eyes now. "But... They came back, but it was only so I could lose them again. For good this time." He was crying feely by this point, the tears tracking down his cheeks. Adam handed him a tissue and he wiped them away, then blew his nose. "There's no fighting them, no defeating them," he said at last, more clearly than anything he'd been saying all night. "You know that, don't you?"

Adam said nothing in return. He couldn't really say that had crossed his mind until the man raised it; he'd been too concerned with gathering information. Only half believing it really, but figuring it would all be great material for the articles, the book, the prize-winning documentary that would eventually end up on Netflix or somewhere.

Fighting Them, if they were real? How would you even…

His thought processes were broken into again when the man started to topple sideways. This time there was no waking him, so Adam just left him to it. He had what he came for anyway, and it wasn't as if he'd be hard to find if he needed more.

Days stretched into weeks, stretched into months. More research, more tracking. Adam even used his holidays, travelling abroad to dig up more on this one subject that was rapidly consuming him. It was during one of these 'missions' that he found writings in an old library in Greece which talked about a device, a crystalline object that might allow communication between men and these 'gods', as it called them, a term Chris Warwick had also used when he'd been in his right—or wrong, depending on how you looked at it—mind. Had Adam been thinking about, what, interviewing *Them*? Had he even been thinking at all? There was no information about how to find it, anyway, so that mystery would have to remain unsolved for now. Some even speculated that it might not be on Earth, but that also did Adam very little good. Similarly, he'd gotten nowhere trying to trace those other folk who either knew about the Controllers' existence or had escaped from them, been part of their number until they broke free and went underground.

All this hadn't gone unnoticed by his editor, of course. He would have been in the wrong line of work if it had. When he questioned his employee about it, Adam simply told him:

"Could potentially be a hot scoop, boss. But I can't really talk about it at the moment."

His editor blinked then, twice. "That's what your uncle said… right before he disappeared."

Adam just stared back.

"It's nothing to do with all that business, is it?"

All what business? Nobody knew what the fuck had happened

to him! But Adam answered truthfully: "No, boss. Nothing to do with that." Not that he knew of, at any rate.

Although he did begin to wonder whether he might suffer the same fate one Friday evening after working late and wandering down into the paper's underground car park. The man who stepped out of the shadows, who was waiting by Adam's old Volvo, nearly gave him a heart attack.

"*Jesus!*" said Adam, backing away from the bloke in the suit, who was wearing an old-fashioned hat, holding up his hands.

"I did not mean to scare you." Then he cocked his head. "Or maybe I did. Maybe you *should* be scared."

"What the fuck are you talking about? Who are you?"

"That doesn't matter, but you need to hear what I have to say."

Adam checked around him then, even bent and checked under the nearby cars. "All right, all right, who put you up to this? Was it Dave? Let me guess, you're supposed to be Deep Throat, right?"

The man looked puzzled, his pinched features scrunching up. "I'm… No, I just came to warn you."

"About a conspiracy? Aliens and all that? Black oil? This is getting old."

"About your investigations into… You need to stop, right now. You're drawing too much attention to yourself. I shouldn't even be here, really. I shouldn't be anywhere near you in case…" It was his turn to look about him. "You have no idea what they're capable of. But I do. I know all too well."

Adam looked at the fellow then, *really* looked at him—took him in. The tightness of his skin, how thin that flesh was, allowing him to see fine veins underneath. There wasn't a hint of hair on that face either, nor at his temples, underneath the hat. The trilby hat to match the antiquated clothing. And those eyes were oh-so blue.

"You're… My God, you're—"

"Please, I don't have much time. You have to promise me you'll back away from this, before it's too late. You're in so much danger."

"Wait, hold on. Let me just get some of this down." An old-fashioned phrase, one his uncle had used back when every reporter carried a notebook around with them and knew shorthand. He was reaching for his phone, about to press the record button when he looked up and saw the person had gone. Vanished, as effectively as his relative had done all those years ago.

Adam rushed over to where the 'man' had been standing, but there was no trace of him. Then he began searching the car park, and it was at this point it happened. A black van, which again came out of the shadows—seemingly out of nowhere—approached him. Adam stood back, allowing it to pass by, but instead it slowed down. The rest was a bit of a blur: the side door opening; men dressed in dark clothing jumping out and grabbing him; the injection that was given to put Adam under; the sound of the door slamming again.

When he came to, he was in a small room. No, not a room—when Adam opened his eyes he saw bars in front of him. He was in a cell… a cage. Chris' words flashed through his mind then:

"*S-S-Sellsss… K-K-Kajjjjjus!*"

And the one thing he'd pronounced clearly: "Pain!" Was that what was coming next? Had this been what the person in the car park had been trying to warn him about? He'd heard about those who served the Controllers on this planet, so perhaps he'd fallen foul of them? Was this where he vanished himself, only to be the focus of conspiracy theories for years to come while he rotted away in here?

He checked his pockets. His wallet, keys, phone—they'd all been taken.

Adam heard footsteps, keys rattling. It looked like he was going to get his answers sooner than he thought. He scrambled to his feet, instantly regretting it when he felt the throbbing in his head. When he almost lost his balance and fell into the wall on the left.

Two of those men dressed in dark clothing were suddenly at the door to his cell, opening it, then motioning for him to come with them. He went, figuring that they wouldn't ask again—not that they had the first time—and would drag him away if he resisted.

They led him to another room, this time with a table in it

and two chairs—a single light bulb illuminating the scene—and gestured for him to sit down. He did so, reluctantly, asking what all this was about. Asking when they were going to let him go. As they walked off, he called after them:

"I have rights! You can't do this!"

He shut up again when another man entered. A man wearing octagonal glasses, his hair greying at the temples. He was holding a clipboard and walked slowly around the table, before taking a seat opposite Adam.

"Look, what's this all about? Who are you?"

He didn't answer Adam's second question—not that he thought the guy would—but did address the first one, after a fashion: "I think you know why you're here, Mr Regis." His tone was flat, emotionless.

Adam swallowed dryly.

"You've been sticking your nose into things that don't concern you," the man went on.

"I haven't—"

"Don't even bother denying it, Mr Regis. We have our sources, the same as you."

I'll bet, he thought.

"The question is, how far down the rabbit hole have you gone? And is there any way back for you?"

"I don't know what you're talking about," Adam informed him.

"Oh, come now, Mr Regis, I think you do. And by the time we're finished here, I'll know everything that you know."

"What if I refuse to tell you, what then?" Adam laughed. "You'll torture me, is that it?"

The man raised an eyebrow. "Wouldn't be the first time."

"You don't scare me," said Adam, but couldn't keep the hitch from his voice.

"Maybe you should be scared."

"Let's just cut to the chase, here." The man put down his clipboard, took off his glasses and breathed on them, before wiping them with a cloth. "I've been hired by a certain body of people to do a job, one I'm very good at. You tell me what you know, and I'll just let you go free."

"Where have I heard that before? Oh yeah, that's right, every single TV show and film where the reporter turns up dead."

"We don't want you *dead*, Mr Regis. That would be more trouble than it's worth, believe me."

And far less entertaining, thought Adam. "I'm not telling you anything. I know my rights."

"Sadly, you don't have any rights. Not really. No-one does. No rights, no freedom. It's all an illusion." He put his glasses back on. "Look, right now there are people going through your apartment, gathering what it's taken you all this time to amass. So this serves no purpose at all."

Adam sat back and folded his arms, said nothing. He was quaking in his boots, but wasn't about to give this bastard the satisfaction of either seeing it or getting anything out of him. Maybe his captor could see that, or maybe the man didn't have as much authority to do what he wanted as he made out, but after what seemed like an age (time seemed to have stood still in that place) they did let Adam go again—and in one piece—dumping him in the middle of nowhere, so he'd had to walk and hitch a lift to a population centre. He was amazed to find, when he got there, he'd only been away for the weekend.

They gave him back his wallet, keys and phone—which had been wiped, as had everything he'd saved in the Cloud. The glasses man hadn't been lying about his apartment, either; every shred of 'evidence' had been taken. All his papers, research, recordings. Everything. Adam thought about calling the police, but what was the point? They hadn't broken in; they'd used his keys. Nothing of any value had been taken, not monetary anyway. They'd left him all of that.

But they'd also left Adam with something else. The knowledge that he was actually onto something. That it was worth pursuing, taking seriously. Not that he hadn't before, it had just stepped up a notch was all.

Worth taking as seriously as the people who kidnapped him obviously did, and the more he thought about it the more Adam wondered whether they were actually in league with the one-eyed ones at all. Or whether they were simply like him, trying to find out as much as they could? And the body of people glasses man had been hired by, who had they been? The government or private individuals? Sometimes they had more power than anyone—all their wealth bought them that.

What was obvious was that if he really intended to go after his story, *if* he really was going to take this seriously, he had to step it up a notch as well.

Like all good reporters, he was going to have to go right to the main source. And that would mean drastic measures.

He'd met someone while looking into OBEs that might be able to help, but even she was reticent. "You're talking about some *Flatliners* shit, here, Adam."

"I know, I know. But will you do it?"

She agreed, but only when he offered her what was left in his savings account—and put it in writing that she wasn't to be blamed if anything went wrong. So, at around three in the morning, he went with her to the basement of St August's, where there were no working CCTV cameras, and Adam Regis let that doctor stop his heart.

It wasn't like Mr Sutton had described, wasn't even like those patients he'd talked to who'd seen the light or looked down on their own bodies. Adam had been there in an instant, transported to their world at the moment of his own death. Deposited directly into the great, blue eye.

He knew pain then, became intimately acquainted with it. But strangely it wasn't his own, it was coming in waves off the others floating around him inside that orb. Millions, *billions* of souls… for that's all they were now, shorn of their physical selves to spend an eternity here. No Heaven, no Hell. No angels or demons. Just this, and the knowledge that—unlike a handful of those who'd put them there—they would never be able to escape.

They were drawn to him, not just because he was new but because he was willing to hear their stories. So many, shouted at Adam to begin with—and simultaneously. Overlapping, jumbled, and constant, so much so that he thought he might go mad. But then he started to separate them, make out their tales of woe. Things that had happened to them which were not just random coincidence but planned, orchestrated. Manipulated. Adam tried to remember them all, but there were just too many and he had no way of recording them.

One that did stick in his mind was the story of Lucy, of her life and the tragic end it came to. Death by fire, leaving her children behind to carry on suffering in her wake. There had been tears in her own eyes when she related it all—Adam wasn't even sure that was possible here, when you were in this state. But she did, she cried... actually cried.

He stumbled upon people that he'd known as well, people he had lost. Relatives like his nan and granddad, cousins, his aunty June on his mum's side. But not his uncle—he wasn't there. He was somewhere else, his fate—if the whispers were to be believed—in the hands of a completely different set of supernatural creatures. Ones the Controllers despised because they had no influence over them or their work: the Order of the Shadows. They had taken his uncle and drained him, used him to become the latest incarnation of the Shadow Writer; the man known as Herbert Lynch.

If he lost track of time when glasses man took him, then it became meaningless there in the great eye. He had no way of counting it, but it felt like he'd been there decades; as long at least as some of the other prisoners who were telling him about their lives.

Then as quickly as he'd arrived in the first place, he felt like he was being scooped out of the eye and was suddenly back in his body once more—the doctor standing over him holding the paddles of her defibrillator. She let out the huge breath she'd been holding.

"Thank Christ!" she said. "Thought I'd lost you permanently there for a moment."

Adam frowned. "How... How long was I—"

"Four minutes or so. Six and you would have been braindead."

He felt like he was anyway, or his brains had been in a blender. Just the lack of oxygen to that particular organ, he was assured. As was anything he might have seen in that state... probably. She still asked him anyway, but he didn't know what to say to her. Couldn't tell her the truth, certainly. And now that he was back, he wasn't sure he could tell anyone else either.

He knew how people like Mr Sutton felt, their reluctance to take anyone into their confidence (change the world? that was never going to happen). Adam jotted down all he could remember from the eye, but now he was home again it just felt like he was chronicling ordinary lives. Without the context of that place, the eye, none of it made any sense—and he still couldn't prove any of it. Knowing what he knew didn't make things any better. It made them a million times worse. The awe, the mystery was gone (teachers? all this had definitely taught *him* a lesson). Even if he did report any of it, he wouldn't be believed—would probably end up somewhere like poor Chris Warwick. So: no articles, no books, no documentaries. To be honest, he was lucky most days to keep his job, especially when he showed up smelling of booze. Adam looked for his drinking buddy in the pubs he frequented, if only to tell him that he knew now why he knocked back scotch after scotch, but he never found him again.

He couldn't even kill himself, because look where he'd end up… (no real escape from *Them*). To his knowledge nobody had ever been plucked from the eye before, so his suffering would probably end up being legendary even there. No abductees had ever returned. (Or had they simply let him return, knowing he could do nothing about any of it?) This place was the only real refuge, but They had their fingers in everything on Earth as well. There was no way to win, there never had been… and no way out. Sometimes he even wished that he had vanished, had winked out of existence; at least then there would be peace.

For Adam, his drive now gone, the best way to exist was just to become numb. To let everything wash over him, because nothing was important anymore. Definitely not the shitty little stories he had to write up day after day; not even the big ones, the hot scoops and major headlines. It wasn't people who created those. They were just a means to an end.

Adam Regis didn't just feel like his life was out of control now, he knew it was. Knew more than just the half of it. And also knew to some extent—no every extent, so completely—that the job, the situation he'd found himself in, the mess he'd ended up in…

Hadn't really been a choice at all.

Reflections

On reflection, he should never have come.

But then reflections were what he was all about. Thinking too much, going over things. Reflections of reflections... stop. Enough. The end.

There wasn't really anyone else who *could* have come, anyway. No one else they wanted or who fitted the bill so precisely. It was like it was always meant to be... if he'd ever believed in fate, that was. Actually it was his old friend, Devereaux, someone he'd met at a conference years back, who had got him involved. He'd done some consulting work in the past for him, so it seemed like a no-brainer—plus who else had the kind of qualifications he had?

Professor Maxwell Strauss, who—in addition to his multiple BScs, MScs, BAs and MAs in a range of subjects—boasted specialisms in Geology, Crystallography and Xeno-Archeology, was the perfect choice to come out here and take a look at what they'd found. What the miners on this planet had found, in fact—and almost destroyed.

No, that wasn't strictly accurate. According to the reports he'd read from the men who'd come across this... this 'artefact'? was that the right word to use?... they had actually drilled into the thing before realising. Thankfully, their laz-cutters had no effect whatsoever on its surface, not even so much as scratching the mirrored material. Anyway, the whistle had been blown and work was halted on the site. Whatever this was, it was so much more important—and valuable—than the ore they'd been tasked to remove from this small moon in the tail end of nowhere. And because the moon belonged to The Corporation, they were the ones who laid claim to the object that had been discovered.

But in what way was it valuable? That was the question. The Corporation usually dealt in cold, hard currency—and surely something that was so durable would be worth a fortune, if they could replicate it, manufacture it somehow. Except not only had it proved impenetrable to their equipment, it also seemed impervious to their scans. Scientists had apparently sat and scratched their heads as gibberish was thrown back at them on their screens. Monitors fizzing and flashing, as if they couldn't cope with the sheer amount of data that was coming through from the examinations, couldn't translate it into something the human mind could understand. Maybe they weren't meant to.

Or maybe it would take a more 'hands-on' approach, the human touch. Computers were all well and good, and were more advanced at this point in history than they had ever been before, but you couldn't beat the observations of a person thinking outside of the box. Or outside of the Prism, in this instance.

For that's what this was, glassy in appearance, four triangles and a square base making up its whole. It had stood out from its unremarkable surroundings like a diamond in the rough. After everyone who had witnessed the discovery had been paid off, or threatened if Strauss knew The Corporation, or even both (there might even have been a mind-wipe or two), an entire base of operations had been set up around the piece. Because they hadn't been able to move it either, no amount of equipment capable of detaching it from its housing.

The object was now contained within a room as white as a supernova explosion, observed through toughened safety glass. Several levels of security stood between it and anyone who might wander into this neck of the galaxy by mistake—nobody ever would, as long as the miners kept their mouths shut. It was to this room Strauss had been delivered after his trip. He hated Elastic travel, so called because it catapulted ships like a stretched and released rubber band, but sadly it was still the only way to be transported such distances. Cocooned in jelly inside virtual coffins, heart rate lowered to an almost deathly beat, it left the person emerging at the other end disorientated, cold… but oddly with a sense of feeling reborn. Strauss would take that, as he could definitely use a clean slate.

As in demand as he was for his work, his private life always had been, and sadly remained, a mess. It was one of the reasons he'd jumped at this gig, even though it would take him away from his university teaching and writing his books for almost a year (Elastic travel was fast, but not *that* fast when the distances were this enormous). There was very little other than his work for him at home, and the prospect of a fresh challenge such as this one—even though he'd been given very little to go on by Devereaux—was too tantalising to pass up.

He wondered if this was how his ancestor, Andrew, had felt when he'd gone into Middletown to examine an entire city that had fallen asleep. He'd been the hero of the hour, stopped the spread of that particular disease, even though it had come at a cost. His great grandfather, who hadn't fathered any legitimate children but hadn't exactly been known for his chastity either. No one really knew what had happened in that city, and because of the nature of the virus Maxwell supposed no one ever would. Quite apart from anything else, the last World War had destroyed many of those records. But it was just another example of how his family line threw up geniuses.

Except Maxwell Strauss was no hero. Quite the contrary. He'd failed to live up to even his father's expectations... Had been weak when he needed to be strong. Just hadn't had it in him, he supposed.

Thoughts, reminiscences, regrets, reflections—they'd all followed him out here to the ends of the universe. He simply couldn't get away from them. But he had the work, and that should be his focus now. The Prism needed to be his focus. And an intriguing puzzle it had proven to be.

He'd heard rumours on the base, chit-chat mainly, once he'd been given the full guided tour, once he'd settled in, and even before seeing the thing itself. Rumours that the Prism 'called' to people... whatever that meant. It hadn't called to Maxwell Strauss, though, hadn't summoned him from Earth for this mission. Hadn't lured him onto the rocks like the Sirens of old did with sailors.

But, when he'd encountered it for the first time, it *had* spoken to him. Actually spoken.

"Well, there it is," Devereaux had said, holding out his hand like a proud parent. "X-425-986. Beautiful, isn't it?"

Strauss had sucked in a breath at the sight of it. He'd never seen anything like it before, not on Earth, nor on any of his other visits to alien worlds—though none as far out as this, it had to be said. "I..." was all he could muster.

Then heard the voice. "*Look*," it said. "*See*."

"What?" he asked, assuming Devereaux had uttered the words.

The man with the shiny bald head at the side of him frowned, puzzled. "I didn't say anything, Max."

"I... I thought I heard—"

"*Look... see...*"

Again, only this time Strauss was staring straight at Devereaux—knew it wasn't him. It wasn't his voice anyway; it was distorted, didn't sound... right. No, those words were inside his head somehow, and in English. Coaxing him to... Strauss turned, walked towards the toughened glass, gazing at the Prism. Even from this distance, it threw back an image of him standing there in his grey flight-suit, which matched the colour of his thinning hair. His wrinkled face was the result of the life he'd led, making him look much older than his 55 years. Devereaux was there too, a little way behind.

But so was something else. Strauss thought he saw a child: a boy, running, playing, laughing. He turned back around, expecting to see the lad in his T-shirt and shorts there, knowing it was impossible, that there were no children out this deep into space—let alone on this moon, in this secret room. He turned back to the Prism, eyes searching for the child—"*Look... see!*"— but it was not inside there either now.

He started when he felt a hand on his shoulder: Devereaux's, as he'd joined him at the observation window. "Are you all right?" his friend asked.

Strauss rubbed a hand across his brow, bent his head and pinched the bridge of his nose. "I... I'm fine. The trip..."

"I understand. Takes a bit out of you, doesn't it? Why don't you grab some food, have a lie down. We can pick this up in the morning," Devereaux told him.

"In the morning," Strauss repeated, then allowed himself to be led from the room—though not without casting a glance over his shoulder first, back towards the Prism.

He'd picked at the rehydrated meal they'd provided, back in his quarters, then attempted to relax; never his strong suit. Sitting in the chair with the book he'd brought—a rare edition of Dickens' *A Christmas Carol*—then laying on the bed, which was comfortable enough but unfamiliar. However, he couldn't get those words out of his head: "*Look... see!*" Couldn't shake the image of that boy; not a reflection at all, but something inside the Prism. Perhaps it had been trying to make contact? Strauss shook his head. Utter nonsense!

Maybe it was an after-effect of the Elastic-drive? He'd heard about cases where people would emerge at the other end and experience hallucinations, aural as well as visual. In some instances they'd never gone away. He covered his eyes with his arm, rolled over on his side. Christ, that was all he needed!

At around three in the morning, and giving up on sleep—that other old friend insomnia greeting him as warmly as Devereaux had when he got here—he found himself wandering the corridors of the base. There were hardly any personnel around, so he felt a bit like a ghost drifting through this world. He had his ID on, his pass which allowed him to access all areas; he was already on the other side of the tight security for this place. So, perhaps inevitably, he found himself back in the room... the anteroom even, a space that historically lead to the treasure. A place where he could observe the treasure that was the Prism, through that glass. Nobody was around in there, either—which meant that he could get a good look at the object without any interruptions.

This he did, moving closer to the toughened glass. Again, the strange triangular surface of the thing threw back an image of him standing there.

"*Look... see!*" he heard again, and cocked his head.

"I... I don't know what you want from me," Strauss whispered, pressing his fingers to the glass, and it repeated its instruction. But to do that, he needed to get even nearer to the thing. Strauss moved sideways, to the door that separated him from the Prism. There was a reader on the side and he took off his ID, waved it in front of the scanner. Time to find out if he really was access all areas… Nothing happened for a second or two, and then the glass door slid sideways. Strauss stepped over the threshold, holding his breath and expecting alarms to go off. They didn't. Nobody had said he couldn't be in the white room with the Prism anyway. It was what he'd been brought here for, after all. To examine this thing, to give his expert opinion.

Tentatively, he walked towards it—towards the triangular side nearest to him.

The reflection of his face grew bigger, multiplied as it bounced off the others. Strauss grimaced, not wanting to see it anymore.

"*Look… see!*"

He shook his head, sick of seeing his visage in the mirror every morning when he could be bothered to shave—he certainly didn't need to be reminded of it here, now, especially like this. Of how old he looked. Of how old he felt… a life heading towards its natural conclusion, more years behind him than in front.

But then something happened. It was almost as if the Prism had read his mind, because the reflection was changing. Lines disappearing, his face growing younger. Strauss held up his hands, peering into the crystalline substance. Closer, closer, until he was repeating the action from outside the room and touching the Prism: getting more hands-on…

Instantly, he was there. On the inside—looking, seeing. Watching. As the reflection grew younger and younger, so young in fact it became that boy he'd witnessed earlier. The one who'd been playing, laughing. T-shirt and shorts. Flitting from swings to roundabout, to slide… A park! The park that wasn't far from their home, the one they always had to pass on their walk to the local shop.

"Max? Maxy…" A woman's voice. One he recognised instantly. Strauss wasn't sure whether he was saying it out loud, or saying it in the vision, but he replied:

"Mum?"

God, could it possibly be…? It had been so long since he'd seen her face and yet here she was, as if it were yesterday, clearer than any memory ever could be. Wearing that green patterned dress she was always so fond of, holding out her hand for him to join her—which he did gladly. He knew that at the end of the trek would be sweets; rationed still, but old Mr Forbes would always hold a few extra back for him. Sweets were better than slides and roundabouts.

And he was having such a fantastic time, out alone with his mother as he liked to be… when it happened. The thing. The good, followed by the bad. The event that triggered everything—cause and effect. His mum had tripped on the pathway, tumbling head over heels, and had just lain there, still, unmoving: a green lump. He could remember the feeling of helplessness, shouting out her name and her not responding, crying and shaking her. The sight of all that blood from the head wound. The world might well have been on the verge of collapse not that long ago—and he'd known nothing about the War back then—but *his* whole world had collapsed when she did.

Eventually, old Mr Forbes had spotted them and rushed to their aid, calling for an ambulance. Then the hospital, his father arriving. So tall, so broad, so strong; ex-military; he'd worked in their R&D departments, their defence departments. Spittle flying from his mouth and catching in his moustache as he shouted at his son to stop crying, to not be so weak. It had only been concern for his wife. Maxwell knew that, looking back, but it hadn't helped.

His mum had woken a few hours later, and he'd been so relieved when they'd allowed him into her room to see her. Concussion, a few bruises. Nothing serious… But it had been enough to plant the seed.

Enough to mean that those bullies at school, like the expert predators they were, smelt the fear, the nerves. All of which fed into the way he was feeling, about himself, about the world. Thinking those thoughts, ones he couldn't get out of his head. It wouldn't be long before his anxiety attacks would start to kick in, the lack of breath, the spasms he couldn't control. For Strauss' father, it was just another sign of weakness, but his mother understood. She was the one who nursed him through it all, arranged for changes in his schooling to foster his love of so many subjects, especially history, science and geography. Another Strauss family genius, if they played their cards right.

It was only when his father collapsed of a heart attack that they found out exactly *why* he'd been so strong all those years. His addiction to stims that masked the symptoms of a rather aggressive form of Barrington's disease, which affected both mind and body. It resulted in him taking his own life because he would rather blow his brains out than show his flaws, than have people think he was frail. His son was too much a coward for that, gladly let people see how weak he was... But had to get stronger if only to help take care of his mum in the aftermath of this tragedy. The insurance paid for home schooling, so he could keep an eye on her—at least until she was feeling a bit stronger herself and insisted that he go back to college. The brain aneurism (a throwback from the fall?) eventually took her away from him, causing more of the panic attacks, more of the seizures. Saw him throw himself into work to take his mind off the fact he was pretty much alone now in the world.

That was the reason why he had all those certificates, because there was nothing else in his life. It was his distraction. The establishments he studied in, and later taught at, were his bubble keeping reality at bay... At least until Rebecca came along. She worked in the office, and they'd bumped into each other after his meeting with a student one day... (clever girl, as well, that Helena Kirby—a standout in his Xeno-Archeology class; he often wondered whatever happened to her). Still shy in the extreme when it came to anything like relationships, he'd bitten the bullet (only not in the same way dad had) and gone on a date with her. Just a drink or two; what was the harm?

That date had led to more, had led to an engagement, had led to marriage. Had led to pregnancy and their son, Harry. He'd had a wobble at that one, the responsibility of it—but had been determined to be the kind of father he'd never had. Supportive, nurturing. As nurturing as any mother.

"*Look... see!*" said the voice again, and Strauss was aware of the fact he was moving round the Prism. Couldn't help himself. Aware that his hands and his face were pressed up against the next triangle as it took him through a guided tour of his life now. A ghost, not just of Christmas past, but of *everything* past.

And he did look—did see as time moved on, as Harry grew and they had a daughter, Maisie. Such a sweet girl, a reflection of her name. They'd been happy as a family, had some good times—but then Strauss had found out about Rebecca and her affairs. "You're always working!" had been the excuse. "Never pay me any attention." But he'd worked *for* the family. Thought he had been enough for her, when clearly he wasn't. Clearly he hadn't been a real man—not strong enough... too weak.

It put a strain on them all, and a separation had been inevitable. Of course, all of this had an affect on his relationship with his kids too—who were now in their teens, Harry preparing to head off to uni himself and Maisie... well, Maisie was getting into all kinds of trouble, hanging out with the wrong crowd, hanging out with boys; like mother, like daughter. Nothing was said, but Strauss couldn't even be sure that they were his children, not after what he'd found out about his spouse. Maybe the affairs had begun even before they'd properly got together? All he knew was that the family that had brought him so much joy was now the source of such pain—the good, then the bad—and he was on the verge of yet another breakdown.

Strauss went to counselling, tried everything from breathing exercises to visualisation: picturing blue skies above all the dark clouds. And meds... those had helped too, even if they had made him feel like a zombie at times. He'd held it together, more or less, but hadn't been able to be there for his son or daughter—felt them slipping away from him, bit by bit, the closeness eroded.

When he came out of the other side of this, they were gone. He barely saw Maisie and when they did speak it always ended in an argument. She never said "You're not my real dad," but the accusation was there in everything she did say. Harry, it transpired, did turn out to be his—but they only found out when he was diagnosed with Barrington's. It had skipped a generation and been passed on to his son, now in his mid-20s and looking at a lifetime in a wheelchair as the disease rampaged through him. Maxwell's weak genes. In the end, Strauss had paid to have him put in suspended animation—a little like the technique they

used for Elastic travel—until a cure could be found, until his symptoms could be reversed. Living but dead at the same time. Another zombie.

Strauss had thrown himself into his work once more and never come up for air after that. Divorce had swiftly followed the diagnosis, so he lived alone… It was better that way, he told himself. He wasn't making a mess of anyone else's life but his own. He welcomed the assignments The Corporation sent his way, just like he'd welcomed this one—to take him away, to help him try and forget. Distractions. Only it hadn't worked out that way on this occasion, had it?

Why? Why show him all this? Past, present? It wouldn't make the future any brighter. He wasn't Scrooge. He'd need the invention of an altogether different writer to sort all of this out, to travel back in time.

"*Look… see!*"

Strauss was conscious of moving around again, of gazing into the third of the triangles—which did exactly that. Took him back and showed him how his life *might* have been. Played a completely different movie, where his mother hadn't fallen that day and his father had never got sick. Where they'd both been proud of him and he'd grown up into a strong, well-adjusted man. Strauss barely recognised himself in fact, but it was him… a version of him anyway; in, what, some parallel universe or something? A version of Strauss who never got the bouts of severe anxiety, who sailed through his education and gained even more plaudits, who met a lovely girl at university called Catherine—his other half in every single way. A woman he trusted and who trusted him, who *completed* him, made him feel stronger than ever—not weak at all. They had two kids as well, one of each the same as before—even had the same names—except they went on to live full and rich lives themselves. Did well in their work and personal lives, with no trace of illness or resentment or—

"*Look… see!*"

"I'm looking… I'm looking, you son of a bitch!" he shouted as he was shown grandchildren visiting at holiday time, Strauss with his arm around Catherine looking on as the kids played in the park near where they both lived. He was in his fifties, but looked so much younger; the consequence of a life lived well. And they both looked so proud...

Tears were streaming down Strauss' cheeks. He didn't know what the purpose of all this served, to show him how life could have been if things had played out differently? Torture, that's what it amounted to, pure and simple. It was too late for him now, no ghost of Christmas... of *anything* to come.

"*Look... see...*" it insisted, and he felt himself shifting or being shifted sideways to the final side of the Prism. "*Behold!*"

Even as he peered into the reflective surface he knew this vision would be different. Knew that it wasn't about him, his life... at least not only about him. Not just his life, but millions... billions more. He was connected to them all in a way nobody else had ever been before, nobody could ever be again. The Prism was making that happen, showing him the world... the worlds, all linked by humanity and its explorations. The universe was opening up to him, unfolding like a flower in bloom. But he was going back in time again, just as he had himself to his first, earliest memories. Only this time he was returning to witness the first memories of everything, to see the moment when it was all created. The famous Big Bang scientists had been talking about and debating for such a long time. It was so pretty, so breathtaking—but over so quickly. A cosmic orgasm and then... life. Stars shining brightly against the blackness of space, planets—some capable of sustaining life, others shunning it.

"*Look...*" came the voice and Strauss could do nothing else, couldn't tear his eyes away from what he was observing now. "*See!*"

He did. He did see, as life on Earth sprang up in the ocean. As humanity slithered onto the beaches from the water. Flashing forward then into apes, into Homo habilis, Homo erectus... Neanderthals overtaken by Homo sapiens; natural selection happening in the blink of an eye. Centuries passing in front of Strauss, all manner of humans, all races and creeds. Strauss watched as civilisations formed, saw the very best and the absolute worst of mankind... sorry, personkind (in this enlightened era of post-equality laws). The ingenuity was matched only by the need for violence, sometimes one following the other.

Strauss saw great wealth and extreme poverty, kindness and hatred, obsession, greed, love and compassion. Everything that made his homeworld what it was, a unique place in the entirety of the universe. Visions of men on the battlefield blended seamlessly with those who tried to cure the sick, with scientists attempting to stamp out viruses. Mushroom clouds and the devastation of the Holocaust tempered with leaps in technology to make lives easier. He saw communications increase, and yet people talking—*actually* talking—to each other less. Saw the world on the brink of a war he'd missed by a hair's breadth, the rebuilding that had taken place afterwards, the setting up of The Corporation—a conglomerate of huge businesses that were the real movers and shakers of the 21st Century. Saw the space race, from the very beginning right up to inventions like Elastic travel. Saw all of this, but still didn't know why he was being shown it, what it had to do with him. Was it all simply another form of communication, through the Prism? Something to do with whoever placed it here, an alien species?

Then all Strauss could see was space. The blackness and the stars inverting, turning inside out. Black specks on a white background, a whiteness that made the room he was standing in—not that he could remember where he was at that point—look dull by comparison. He was in another place, on the other side of somewhere else. And he had no more time to marvel at the strangeness of it all, which made some of the trips he'd been on when taking his meds look like… like a walk in the park. No more time, because he was aware of his consciousness moving forwards—being dragged if the truth be known.

"*Look… see. Behold!*" said the voice.

He *was* looking, but it made no sense. Strauss was passing through a thick fog, almost a living mist. A barrier, closing this place off from everything else. He was drifting over another world; one so different to his own yet connected in a way he didn't fully understand. A darker reflection. Huge cities populated this reality, flanked by volcano-like peaks which belched out fire rhythmically. But a fire that somehow Strauss knew held no heat—quite the reverse, its coldness representative of this world's lack of warmth, of feeling.

Just as he'd had no choice but to come here in the first place, now he was pulled down into one of those cities. There shadowy creatures drifted, moving from one location to the next; floating above the streets, which twisted and turned, snaking into each other.

The figures were hooded, but there was something about those hoods—like they were an extension of them, the same as the cloaks that wafted about their person yet at the same time moved independently of the creatures they were attached to. The Prism zeroed in on one of the shapes, and Strauss went with it: trailing one of the figures to its destination, a massive tower where it would find a nook in which to position itself: an organic seat rising up out of fungi-like walls when they sat.

Clear orbs, that looked like crystal balls, detached themselves form the walls and began to hover around the creature in the hood. They looked to be made of the same substance as the Prism—so maybe that was it, Strauss reasoned. Maybe they'd left this here after all in order to reach humanity? And yes, as he continued to watch he saw that this figure was in fact watching *them*. Visions etched on the orbs, the same as he'd seen; his visions… his reflections. They were observing *his* species, had been watching right from the start.

No, not observing. Because the more he scrutinized, the more he got a sense that this thing was directing the events in the orb. Manipulating them, interfering with his species rather than just observing from the sidelines.

"*Look… see!*"

But Strauss didn't want to anymore. He was getting the message, knew why he'd been shown a rerun of his life, and what might have happened had these bastards not been messing with him… (making a mess). Messing with them all! Indeed, just to hammer it home he saw the boy in the T-shirt and shorts, the boy he'd been. Saw the twitch of a gnarled finger, a glow coming from beneath that hood, this monster causing his mother to fall.

Dominoes falling. Cause and effect. Fate… Distractions.

All leading him to this moment, this trip. The Prism hadn't needed to call to him. It was all predetermined; *controlled.* He'd had no say in the matter. It was as he thought this that the creature seemed to turn, to sense his presence. To *see* him!

It peeled back the hood that was a living part of it, revealing a hideous face: thin, veiny flesh, bones protruding; and a single cerulean eye in the centre of its forehead. The source of the glowing. Strauss didn't want to see, but again couldn't look away—as he was drawn into the eye. As he was shown the thing that he assumed was their god: a massive version of that eye in the centre of their world, meaty tendrils running from its edges, things floating underneath its surface. Figures, people…

Ghosts.

That's what they looked like, spirits screaming and trapped beneath. Feeding it somehow, more joining it all the time once its… its children, those…Controllers had finished with them.

So many lost souls.

"*Behold!*" the voice said finally—was it the Prism or the creature?—and Strauss knew then the name of this thing. *The Beholder.*

He wanted to ask why? So many questions… Not least of which why he'd been allowed to see it, why the Prism had shown him, given him the message? Did it want him to do something about it all? If so, what? He didn't stand a chance against monsters like these.

But perhaps he was being shown so he could at least warn the others? If that was the case, he needed to break this connection—return to the white room. To Devereaux. Maybe there was a way to reach this other place using Elastic travel? Perhaps the Prism itself could be used as a weapon? For once in his life, he had to be strong. He had to be the hero.

For a second or two it seemed like he was being granted his wish, because he was moving back out of the eye, that mirror of their god, was back in the chamber with the Controller… Only it was pointing at the orb, showing him another vision. Another reflection.

"*Look... see!*"

A vision of him in the white room, on the floor next to the Prism, shaking. The anxiety attack that he was having was massive, the knowledge far too much for him. Thinking those thoughts, ones he couldn't get out of his head. Strauss could hear the beating of his heart, so loud now, so fast. Saw Devereaux and the others rushing in, just like Mr Forbes had done so long ago—the man commenting that Strauss shouldn't even have been able to gain access to the Prism on his own.

"There... there wasn't anyone else..." Strauss was mouthing, realising his importance; that he'd had another mission entirely, and that his weak body was failing him. That he was failing everyone. "They didn't want anyone else... Please... look!" He was pointing at the Prism.

Devereaux followed his gaze but shook his head. "I... don't see anything, Max."

"Look, see..." Jabbing his finger with the last of his strength. Then sighing. "Don't... don't let me die."

"Jesus, where are those medics?" Devereaux shouted.

"Don't..." Strauss managed. "Please don't..."

"*Look, see...*" the voice echoed a final time, and he realised it was his own. "*Behold...*" Unable to finish the name as the beats reached a crescendo. (They never would have believed him anyway.) As Strauss' head dropped, and he saw his reflection once more in the Prism, stretching back and through the crystal, bouncing off each side. On and on, never-ending. Trapped, like he would be soon; on the other side. In the eye. Reflections, all reflections.

Reflections of reflections of...

Stop. Enough.

The end.

They Watch

Is it out of our hands? you ask.
Life, love, death—existence.
The daily ritual of being, just being.
A constant round of disappointment,
Of fear.
And like the show says, 'Trust no one.'

No control; is it fate...
Or something else? Something more?
They have Their Eye on you.
Go about your business, but going nowhere.
Puppets, you feed them: a 'simple life'.
Entertainment for these 'gods'.

Time, space: it means nothing,
To Them.
Transcends the borders,
Straddling the reality between two worlds.
One of green, blue, white. The other,
Hidden.

Mist, unnatural fog and beyond,
Lie the secrets.
All the answers are here,
To every question you've ever put.
Why are we born, why do we die?
Why so much pain, heartache and...
Suffering?
Why?
Why?
Why?

Dominion.

A city: the towers alive.
House beings that decide,
Our every thought and action.
Our destiny.
It will be too late to turn back.
To pretend it isn't real,
Once you know the truth.
Once you've seen that...
Cerulean orb. Thick, throbbing veins.
Behold.

A grand plan, or a twist.
Weaving life's rich tapestry.
And its children, those cyclopean things,
'Control'.

And They watch,
And They watch,
And They wait.

Bonus Material

Story Notes

Astral

'Astral' was something like the sixth or seventh professional short story I ever wrote in 1998, and by professional I mean writing with an aim to having it published somewhere as opposed to just tinkering around at home for fun. Paul Bradshaw was just starting out with *The Dream Zone* and asked me to do a story for him. The tale was later also included in the 2003 trade paperback edition of John B. Ford and Simon Clark's book, *The Derelict of Death & Other Stories*. I've been interested in out of body experiences for a long time, ever since I saw a programme on the subject when I was in my teens. A number of excellent stories exploring this theme had already been written, but I was desperate to include it in one of my own tales. So to make it a bit different, I combined this with another idea I was developing at the time: that of a race of beings who manipulate and control mankind from behind the scenes, with a power over life and death, thought and desire, nature and reason. Who would have thought I'd still be writing about them all these years later?

Like so many other people—even the rich and famous, and the supposedly happy—I've had seriously bad patches in my life. There have been times when everything has gone wrong, when I've felt like asking, 'Why me?' I've also experienced the feeling that certain things have happened because they were meant to be. Call it fate, call it God or whatever. So what I was trying to do with The Controllers was present another possible explanation for this, and for the terrible tragedies we see on the news each day. I suppose it absolves us of the responsibility to some extent, but it's also quite frightening when you think about it. Especially when I tell you that I wrote the story in just a few short hours, almost as if someone—or something—was telling me what to put.

From the staggering, and heartening, reaction I've had to 'Astral' it would seem I'm not the only one who thinks like this. Who believes it's all out of our hands. That we're simply living out a story someone else has written. And that a race of unfathomable creatures living in another reality created by a gigantic all-seeing eye (which I later dubbed *The Beholder*) might, just might, be running the show.

Eye of the *Beholder*

This is a story that's been reprinted a few times, most recently in my 'best of' collection *Shadow Casting* from SST. In my defence, it's a tale I'm seriously proud of. It's one of the few that really got to me as I was writing it, the character of Lucy becoming so real that by the end it actually upset me to kill her off. Maybe she did exist out there somewhere, maybe you even knew her? Whatever the case, she didn't deserve what those damned Controllers put her through. But then again, who does? It's also the first story in which the giant Eye gets its name. I think it is an appropriate one, because its nature is to observe. To *behold*. And never interfere.

The Pain Cages

This is an odd one, as you'll probably know if you've read it. I'm struggling to remember exactly where the jumping off point for this novella (which was originally written on request for Books of the Dead) came from but I think it was reading a magazine article about the kinds of things you might go through if you had a brain tumour. The paranoia that might build up, the hallucinations, the changes in behaviour... I really wanted to put all this into a story at some point, and ended up doing two parallel timelines for it. The first is a kind of kidnapping tale, which you don't realise until the end is about the operation to try and save Chris Warwick's life. The second is the span of years leading up to that event, after an incident that happens when he's very young which may or may not have triggered it in the first place. Whether his notions about The Controllers are real—the tumour allowing him to 'see' them—or are just symptoms of his sickness I left ambiguous in 'The Pain Cages'. Though, as you'll see as you read on, all these years later I finally had to pick a lane in order to write one of the new stories for this collection.

Secrets

I handwrote this story even before 'Astral', but never felt happy enough with it to send it anywhere. Then I found it again in a drawer when I was looking for a bonus extra story for my *Disexistence* collection a couple of years ago. In that one it was presented as a curiosity and to some extent should still be regarded as one, but I feel it's only right for the tale to take its proper place now in this collection, especially as I've linked all the others together. It wears its influences on its sleeve, *Hellraiser* being chief amongst them. Although my creations don't wait for people to call them, they're around at your birth, directing you, eradicating your free will. It was originally called 'The Secret', then changed to 'The Controllers'—but for this collection I've renamed it simply 'Secrets', as that's what it's about.

The Scoop

Okay, here we come to the first of the new stories in this collection—which I actually wrote last. You'll find out why in a second, but essentially it fits chronologically into the collection as a whole at this point and draws together everything from 'Astral' to 'Secrets'. The older I get, the more I like to revisit stories I did earlier on in my career. Might just be that I like dropping in on characters I haven't 'seen' in while to find out how they're doing. Usually not well, I have to say. I recently did it with *Flaming Arrow*, which catches up with Robert and co. from the *Hooded Man* trilogy a few years after the last book, *Arrowland*. I also did it with *RED*, but set the sequel—*Blood RED* from SST—only moments after the first. But, anyway, this collection seemed like a good opportunity to find out what happened to the people in The Controllers tales after the fact. Not only that, I decided to tie it in with a story I wrote around the same time as 'Astral' in that first batch when I was hoping to become a professional fiction writer. 'Shadow Writer'—most recently published in my 'Best of…' collection *Shadow Casting*, already mentioned—was one of my first published stories, but also gave me the name of my website and a couple of anthologies I did back in the day. That followed Stephen Regis (see if you can spot the gag), who becomes the legendary titular writer at the end; while 'The Scoop' follows his nephew, as he develops his own particular obsession. It's just another way of saying nothing ever happens by chance, and that cause and effect wins the day. Bonus points, by the way, if you spotted my character The Torturer from the story of the same name (most recently seen in my collection *Nailbiters* brought out through Black Shuck Books and in the novel *Deep RED*, which caps off that trilogy). He gets about a bit, that's for sure…

Reflections

This tale was actually written specifically for an anthology a couple of years ago where Prisms were the focus. It didn't end up going in that, but did give me a chance to write about The Controllers in the future; and allowed me to hint at the Prism here in 'The Scoop' as part of Adam's research. Back then I was also writing a novella—which turned into a short novel—that was an SF/horror hybrid called *Planet of the Dead*. At the time of writing this note I have no idea whether that one's seen the light of day or not, but it did allow me to put a few nods to it in 'Reflections' (such as Elastic Drives, The Corporation—which is the culmination of the Torturer's group from 'The Scoop'— and a mention of Helena Kirby, who's the protagonist of *PotD*). The more observant amongst you will also have figured out that Maxwell Strauss is the ancestor of Andrew from another short novel of mine, *Sleeper(s)* (recently reprinted in *Kane's Scary Tales* from Steve Dillon's Things in the Well publishing company). Here I finally show the extent of The Controllers' meddling and how far back it goes, whilst at the same time hammering home just how futile the fight against them is… or is it? That, I haven't really decided—and maybe I might come back to it at a later point. Then again, I might not. As fantastical as the idea of The Controllers is (or do they just want you to think that?) there's something very grounded and realistic about the lack of happy endings their tales offer. Laugh-riots they are not. Perhaps, when you get right down to it, that's why they've proved so popular over the years and why this collection exists in the first place.

They Watch

This was part of a clutch of poems I was asked for when editor Peggy J. Shumate was putting together a hardback book of horror poetry, *Cemetery Poets: Grave Offerings*. I'd already written a couple of stories about the Controllers by then, and those were still quite fresh in my mind. So I thought I'd draw on them as the subject for at least one of those poems—others included 'The Ugly', which was reprinted in the British Fantasy Award-nominated *Monsters* from Alchemy Press, and 'Stalking the Stalker' which more recently appeared again in my crime/psychological collection *Nailbiters*. I don't do much poetry, but I did enjoy penning these so maybe I'll return to it one day.

Early Handwritten Version of 'Astral' - 'Astral Hearts' (circa 1997/8)

Astral Hearts

Curse or
Bless ~ don't know
- wait ou you're
heart story 1st

(1)

astral

I first discovered I had the ✓ talent at an early age, purely by accident. It was my misfortune (or fortune, depending on how you look at it) to be struck down with a fever as a youth. I spent a week in bed, the sweat pouring out of my ~body~, so that the sheets around me remained perpetually soaked. And during this time I dreamt I was pulled up and out of my body; I spent many hours simply watching myself restlessly tossing around on the bed below. I know I probably should have been frightened by the experience, but I wasn't. Indeed, I began to enjoy it - welcoming the opportunity to view myself as others saw me; as my mother looked upon me sat by my bedside, a cloth in her hand.

When the fever lifted I assumed the dreams had been caused by my illness and said nothing to my family. After all, many bizarre visions had passed before my eyes during those seven days, things that couldn't possibly be real. Or so I imagined at that ~time~ age.

It wasn't until some considerable time later that I realised I hadn't been dreaming when I went on my limited excursions, at least not in the same way most people perceive the notion.

Bored one night when sleep was proving elusive, I thought how wonderful it would be to float outside of myself as I had done when the fever gripped me. I missed the feeling of freedom it gave me; the knowledge that I was no ~longer~ held back by the matter which encased me, ~and so~ I closed my eyes, and willed myself upwards. To my astonishment it started to happen again. I felt the separation - it is not painful at all, but there is a mild sense of loss - as my ethereal form drifted towards the ceiling.

Though it was dark, I could see myself quite clearly in the bed. I looked asleep, peaceful and resting quietly. For a while I watched myself breathing in and out again, just like the last time. But then I began to wonder... Could I move outside of the room? I had no physical ties, so surely it was possible. All I had to do was will myself on.

I tried to clutch at the door handle, but instead found that my hand went straight through the door itself. Cautiously, I followed suit, and soon I was moving through our house.

I glided over my parents, asleep in the next room - then paid a visit to my Grandfather who was staying with us for the holidays. There was no way, of describing what it feels like if you haven't got the talent yourself: no one who has only walked the earth would fully understand, and I get stronger.

As time went on, I began to experiment more and more with my power. No longer was I restricted to the house; I could roam around unhindered across the country side, past towns, villages, cities. I saw as much of life as I could, and never once did I have to leave my own bedroom.

Anyone who saw me lying on the bed, would conclude that I was having a nap or perhaps even meditating - when in actual fact I was touring the dales, examining every aspect of this planet. Every day I would go just a little further, testing the limits of my abilities. I always knew when I had strayed too far, because I would feel strange pangs - a desperate need to be back in my human shell once more.

It was my secret, and I never revealed it to anyone (not even my beloved Jessica). I feared not just the taunts of people who didn't believe, but also the attentions of people who did believe - who would seek to use me for their own ends. No, I travelled alone and kept the knowledge to myself. It was not in my nature to spy - heavens, in all the years I have been doing this, not once have I intruded upon another person's privacy. Not on purpose, at any rate.

By my mid-twenties I had been around the world, as well as journeying to its very core. It was incredible passing through solid substances like a ghost. I could see molecules which made up the things we take for granted - plants, rocks, earth. I simply stepped inside and there they were, roaming around me, as energetic as tiny mites.

There was nowhere left to go but up. I had long since mastered the act of flying, soaring with the birds in the open expanses of blue and white. It was joyous beyond compare to see the world from so many miles up.

And beyond the wide blue yonder lay the heavens. A black curtain with white specks, pinpricks of light from a seemingly invisible light force.

That's when I began to sense them.

As I pushed further on into the stars, things came out to me - subconsciously or not I couldn't tell, but I could definitely feel their presence out in space. Initially I only heard their moans and I wasn't able to

* (I once spent [?] of myself in a glass shop front - or coloured reflections

* or me up a mountain side

* as if an invisible piece of elastic was tied to my leg, ready to snap me back at any time.

daff

illumination

800

It was fascinating. I loved to pass by these twinkling dots. I felt truly at home amongst the stars, though I never strayed too far without the pangs nudging in.

But the older I got, the further I could go. I played upon the surface of the moon, visited the warlike planet of Mars and danced through the rings of Saturn and ....

I felt like a god in the realm of the gods. How little I knew.

The day would come when I strayed too far out into the depths, where reality began to mix with fantasy. Colours spiralling into infinity and beyond — a wild cacophony of weird music reverberating in my ears. Stars and space ran into each other like paint until all that was left was a swirling caleidoscope around me.

That's when I began to sense them.

It will come as no surprise to those amongst you with open minds, that there are higher forces at work in the universe. But quite what form these "powers" take are beyond even the most creative imaginations.

As I pushed further out, something called to me. Subconsciously or not, I couldn't tell, but I could definitely feel a presence — I found it easy enough to slip through dimensions, as easy as I found it to move through granite or soil. I simply willed myself to follow the summons, while realising where it would take me.

Naturally, I didn't make it all the way in one session. I was not strong enough to break through at first. But eventually I came upon their plane of existence.

It was like swimming through dense fog, yet not fog — More like living strands of tissue which whipped around my form, touching me, trying to cocoon me in its web. I almost turned back, but the summons was much louder & it increased in volume the deeper into the "fog" I plunged. And there was not just one entity calling to me but many, a unified chorus of voices pleas. It was painful to hear but, as so often happened, my curiosity got the better of me and I could do nothing except soldier on.

Ultimately I broke free of the tissue to emerge upon a strange land. Barren ground stretched out as far as the eye could see, there was no horizon to in sight; the sod, dark maroon in colour, carried on forever.

The ground gave me some sense of direction on that "world", although I soon realised I had to pass into the very earth to reach them.

And as I made my way into the warm room, I felt fear. Never before had I been afraid while I was in this state; what could hurt me when my body was in another place? That was no longer true here, I reasoned, and it wasn't long before I found out why.

I travelled to a pulsating heart at the centre of the kingdom. It was round and bright red with a shiny surface. Again I saw my reflection, this time in the heart's surface. Each time it throbbed, I shook visibly.

There were veins, pumping tubes, which lead from the heart to... I could scarcely believe what I was seeing. Each of the millions - perhaps even billions - of veins were connected to eliptical holes in the cavern's sides. And every single cleft is filled with a human form - blue and almost transparent like my self.

The people there are bound to the sides of the walls by a substance that resembles black tar. It oozed over them, and appeared quite alive. So many victims provide a life force so the heart can continue to pump. It was they who called to me over the vastness of space. Their misery and eternal torment I could sense - The dead spirits of my own world.

[You've] been here yourself, in your dreams. Or, you may have cast it from your mind when you awoke, the strangeness of the place at odds with your own view of reality, but I assure you you have been here - seen this as I once did when the fever brought me down as a child. However, the dreamer is only a visitor here, not a captive. That doesn't come until much later.

One voice among the wrong space was louder than the rest to me. I headed towards it, a sweet sound now corrupted by this detestible atmosphere. It wasn't until I was almost upon the coles, that I recognised the voice of my sister Jessica. Her face was upturned and I could swear I saw a tear trickling glass-like down her cheek.

With a determination I'd never felt before I tried to rip away the slime that held her, and attempted to pull the heart's suchry out of her chest. Neither would budge an inch.

Behind me, the heart was stirring. I turned to witness several things pushing through the surface. They broke; wings beating in an effort to chase me. All were corpulent creatures, the colour of weak Cider.

~~Story~~ ~~really~~ hards

I avoided the ~~nearly~~ line ~~coming~~ of the first, only by flying backwards over its head so that it ~~still~~ ~~struck~~ the kingdom wall.

Jessica's eyes ~~were~~ followed me as I dodged a second and a third. If they could see me, then they could probably hurt me too.

Before I could see it, one of the heart's vein's was coming at me, heading right for my chest. To my surprise, I found I could catch hold of it with both hands and halt its progress. It was strong, but I ~~was~~ succeeded in twisting round and hurling it at one of my attackers.

The vein ripped straight through it and out the other side.

I ~~so~~ went back to Jessica, ~~and~~ ignoring the other beasts heading in my direction — but before I got there ~~could reach her~~ I felt those all too familiar pangs. My time was up and I felt myself being pulled back — my earth bound body staking its claim on my soul. I held out a hand to her and then I was ~~once~~ yanked through the mist. My last recollection ~~before~~ waking up was of Jessica's ~~longing~~ face, pleading with me to free her.

Since that day I have made innumerable attempts to reach the kingdom of the astral heart, that great ~~or~~ reaper of beings at the centre of its very own universe. I have failed every time.

But I am an old man now, and I know that my end is fast approaching. On that day I will rise from my body a final time and will not be able to answer it again.

I will pass by the stars again, no doubt escorted by the maggot-bugs, ~~and~~ ~~I~~ ~~will~~ ~~be~~ ~~taken~~ ~~-~~ ~~as~~ nervously ravished to the heart. ~~me all will be — to~~ ~~the heart.~~ ~~may away~~

At least I ~~will~~ ~~and~~ see Jessica again, even if it means we will ~~be~~ ~~struck~~ together in perpetual horror.

Handwritten Changes to 'Astral Hearts' as 'Astral' (circa 1998)

ASTRAL - CHANGES ①

It was like I was being pulled sideways through dimensions
- Reality no longer existed for me any more, as the strands
of time just wrapped around my astral form. But still
I followed the calls, regardless of their destination. I
felt compelled to do so.

When I finally broke through the veil I came upon a
place unlike any other. A city with towering black
buildings and twisted, intricate streets. I was high
above it, observing from afar the dots which moved along
the gaps between buildings: black beetles gracefully walking toward
their destinations.

I did not fear cold - how could I when my body was
elsewhere? - but I shivered nonetheless. What was this panorama
a? where was I

Ignoring my trepidation, I plunged myself towards the
megalopolis, always following the summons. The closer I
got to the steeples, those glistening protrusions, the
more I could tell they were not made from any substance
once known to man. The surface of the buildings
pulsed, and I saw thick tubular veins running up
the side. I couldn't be sure, but it looked as if
the buildings were organic, alive in some way. I could
swear the whole city was looking at me, through me...

Wandering along the streets, I found my unease growing.
The figures too small from above soon came into sharp
focus on the ground level. They were hooded beings who
kept to the darkness, shrouded in secrecy. But their
cloaks too seemed to cling to them, floating around each
one like a second skin.

I watched them striding along their weird and twisted
streets: some in pairs, always in trios - They went about
their hidden business, gliding from structure to structure,
heads bowed, chanting insane mantras foreign to my
ears.

I decided to trail a pair inside, staying a comfortable
distance behind. Imagine my confusion at witnessing such sights,
as the creatures made their way to hallowed arcanes
- each with space enough for one person. When they bent to
sit down, seats sprang up from underneath, actually growing
from the floor to oblige them. I now firmly believe the
material was responding to some form of mental command -
Globes the size of postures detached themselves from
their surroundings around these hooded figures, float about their
heads. I could see pictures on the spheres, burred at
first then stranger and stranger. Each image was of a

sometimes on
different parts of my world (places I had been, people I had
encountered) - They were observing my home t, just I was
observing theirs, undisturbed, constantly ... but for what
purpose?

Then I noticed that the figures' hoods were glowing a
strange azure colour, and every time one of them reached
up a withered, pale hand something changed on the
"screens". A man would stop and go up a street he never
set out to explore, a woman would instantly fall in love with
someone she'd only just met (to the point of possession),
a doctor prescribes the wrong medicine to his patient (with
catastrophic results), a climber decides to take on just
one more mountain (his last)...* A plethora of minutae, details
upon details upon details - Decisions "controlled" somehow
by this mysterious race. I realised then, that there must
have been billions of globes in each tower, and that
these Controllers (for want of a better word) were in charge.

*A military
leader
believes
it is
sure to
use deadly
force.
A husband
crosses
that
moment
to murder
his wife

A terrible thought occurred to me at that moment - If
these unspeakable creations had a hand in every part of
our lives, were manipulating and guiding each human's
destiny - what was their goal in doing so? And how long
had this been going on for - how long had we been
just playthings to them? All the beauty in the world
the stars, the heavens, were simply a back drop for
some machiavellian scheme - we were like cattle in a
field, herded onwards, told when to eat to sleep ... My god
who were these people?

The call came again, disturbing my thoughts - it was
much more anxious this time and I could do nothing but
leave these Controllers to their affairs.

Outside again I passed over more of the living city,
until I came to a great ellipse of what appeared to
be water - cool, blue liquid in a gigantic lake. The voices
came from that location and I dived down to hover by
its side. Up close I could see that although the
surface of the lake was rippling, it wasn't any kind
of water I recognised. Indeed, there was a film over
the top which vibrated lightly, and I saw more of
the worm-like veins around its massive edge - set in
the slimy ground so that to resemble a rare mineral
floating in oil.

Suddenly the surface shifted and I could see things
moving about beneath. I took these to be monstrous
things at first glance, but as they rose up I could
see instead they were people - faces, bodies - all
human, but different. There was nothing tangible about

128

them; they were outlines — souls perhaps? And these were the haunted inhabitants who had called to me — trapped in the blueness with little hope of escape. And there, almost submerged by the others, was the countenance of my dear sweet sister Abigail. Though I could not be sure I thought she mouthed the words "help me", before being pushed aside by more of the orbs' residents.

I was just about to head inside after her when a thin blackened fresh snapped over the eclipse. Within seconds it had moved back again, and there was no sign of the people beneath.

I knew then that this was a living eye, which had just blinked. The source of all that power flashed unlike and more visions passed through my mind — I was being shown things, incredible things I could never explain about the purpose of all this... about the controllers. The eye transferred its information to me at speed...

But the flow was broken by several of the hooded ones appearing at the eye's rim. This time they could see me, they knew I was here. More poured over, and more, and still more. Until there was a swell of controllers around the eye.

In unison, they peeled back their hoods — and I just got a quick glance of their appearance before terrific pain set in. The hoods, as I had guessed earlier, were a living part of them — They peeled back like a scab on a spot to reveal almost transparent flesh with criss-crossy lines visible underneath. They were hairless and in the middle of their brows was a blue eye — just like the larger one they all gathered around.

It was the light from the eyes — a combined effort — which I found too much to endure. I still don't know to this day how I could actually feel the knives of burning hot agony every chance into me, but I assure you it was quite real at the time, and intense enough to cause me to lose consciousness after only a couple of seconds.

The next thing I knew I was awake on my bed. I can only imagine that my body chose that precise moment to pull me back, and thus I escaped the fate those bastards had in mind for me.

Or perhaps they let me go intentionally — knowing I could never tell another soul of the things I'd seen without risking confinement to an institution. One thing I do know for sure, they wiped my mind in some way so fast, I can't remember what the great eye told me. And with each passing day the events become more muddled in my mind (hence the reason for writing this account* — which I have instructed my lawyers to release upon my death).

Also, try as I might, I cannot find my way back to their reality — in my travels now I am restricted to our own plane, as once I was to my parent's house. Only ... in my sleep, in my nightmares do I see the place again, though I'm damned if I can remember much when I wake up.

Yet I know that one day I will return, on the day that I rise up from my body and cannot find my way back. And on that day I will become part of the great eye with my sister, feeding it in some way, wrapped in the blue. Its secrets will be told to me once more, but by then it will be too late.

I just hope that before I end up there I'm allowed a few brief moments to look upon my world, and to dance amongst the stars* as I did before I discovered the truth.

Perhaps then I might take that astral place with me — and remember it when all else seems pointless...

130

Early Handwritten Version of 'The Controllers'/'The Secret'/'Secrets' (circa 1996/7)

The Controllers

I could tell as soon as he walked through the door, that he wasn't your average visitor to Mick's place. - it was discovered, granted and a bit. For a start he wore a suit, dark grey and well pressed, And his shoes were a little too shiny for their own good.

But the man himself, well that was a different matter. The pale skin was stretched tight over his face, especially at the cheekbones which threatened to break through at any moment, and receding hair was slicked back; plastered to his scalp.

And those eyes, my God! when he looked around the bar, you could feel the chill going through the regulars - the few that were still there, that was.

Then they settled on me? I felt them boring into my head, piercing blue and white orbs wielded with the skill of a hypnotist. I tried to look away, but couldn't.

In the end it was the man who broke the stare. He approached the bar, small steps at first, then bigger strides. He placed a bony hand on the polished counter and leant against it. I remember thinking he'd probably fall down if that crutch prop had been removed.

Shirl at the other end of the bar, kept her distance. She had no intentions of coming near, let alone serving this guy, and I couldn't say I blamed her.

Yet something about him was fascinating to me, don't ask me what, or why. Finally I plucked up courage to speak.

"What'll it be?" I said, hoarsely.

He stared at me again and replied in a strong, deep crumpled voice, "Scotch. I'll be over in the corner booth." + he left a fiver on the bar

My palms were sweating as I fixed his drink and watched him make for his table. I heard the bones in his knees crack when he slid onto the green leather bench.

He looked up again as I brought the Scotch over. "There you go, is that all you want?"

He nodded.

"Okay, well enjoy your drink." I was just about to turn my back / leave the table when he grabbed my arm. I was so startled, "Really, I can't I nearly dropped the tray I was carrying.

I'm worry - "Sit down," he whispered. There was no threat in his imitation and the grip on my arm wasn't particularly strong - how could it be with those frail hands - but all the same I obeyed his order. Maybe it was something those eyes again; maybe he was a hypnotist of some kind, "Sit down," I don't know.

- But, the bar was pretty quiet that Thursday and Shirl could handle any

"What do you want from life William?" he asked matter of factly.

I gaped open-mouthed at the stranger, "How do you know my name?"

He simply closed his eyes and ~~inquired~~ again. To my surprise I found myself answering.

"I guess to be happy, have a bit of cash in the bank that sort of thing."

"No, that's not it, at all," he snapped, "Tell me what you really want."

"I don't –"

"Isn't it true you want to wake up with Hannah beside you again? To take your son to ~~the~~ ball game again - watch him grow up?"

every morning for the rest of your life.

"Now you wait a minute, who sent you? ~~Hannah Are you.~~ ~~Hannah's lawyer or something.~~ A private dick ~~she's sent to spy on me? What?~~"

Now I was angry.

He laughed, and that just made me more upset.

"~~No, I've got nothing to do with your wife. At least not directly.~~"

~~Anger changed to puzzlement as I listened to the man's story, and which he told me did very little to ease my confusion.~~

~~He was at the bar, he said, and needed somewhere inconspicuous - to hole up for a night or two. He seemed to know all about me, as the crummy apartment I called 'home' since the split~~

"Calm yourself William"

"You look like a man with problems. I know how you feel." he said matter of factly. "Perhaps you'd like ~~to~~ ~~tell~~ me what's troubling you." *share with*

I opened my mouth to ~~say~~ ~~something to~~ stick it, but to my surprise ~~I~~ began ~~telling to~~ him about Jadine. *because tell him where he could*

"It only happened the ~~once~~," I ~~blurted~~ ~~stared~~, "let's get that straight from the start. I'm not one of those playboys that ~~you~~ ~~see~~ come in cruising for skirt, no sir!"

"I know," the man said reassuringly. *William*

"How did you –"

"Please," he interrupted, "continue."

I looked sideways at the stranger and carried on, *he seemed*

It was about three weeks ago now. I was working late ~~that~~ ~~but~~ when this woman comes in. She ~~was~~ was very good looking, and I'd be lying if I said I hadn't noticed her, because I had. Anyway she sat down on that stool over there," I thumbed behind me to show him where I meant, "and ordered a ~~cocktail~~ martini."

"You were attracted to this woman?"

"Sure, like I said, she was very pretty. But I

The Controllers

For a start he looked neat:

I could tell as soon as he walked through the door, that he wasn't your average visitor to Mick's place. His suit ~~looked~~ was ~~too common~~, ~~and~~ well pressed, and his shoes were too shiny for their own good.

~~Receding hair was slicked back and plastered to his scalp, and his complexion was pale. In fact he looked ~~older~~ He,~~

But the man himself, well that was a different matter. ~~He could see~~ His cheekbones were — and deathly breaking to burst through what looked like wafer-thin pale skin. ~~Sunken ~~shadow~~ stared under~~ ~~his eyes~~

didn't really .... that is, I didn't go out of my way to talk to her, you know."

"Yes."

"In fact it was Jadine who, for that was her name, Jadine, - she was the one who started talking to me. She was ~~pretty~~ down because she'd just lost her job at the mall. I guess she'd come to drown her sorrows, and let me tell you she did some drawing that night."

"This Jadine, you spent the night with her didn't you?"

"Listen Pal, I don't know why I'm even —"

"Answer." he snapped. And I felt compelled to do so.

"Yeah, alright! We went back to her place after the bar closed."

"And you never thought what it might do to Hannah ~~if~~ when she found out?"

"Of course I did, I was just ~~too~~ mean ~~that is all~~ —" I stopped in mid stream. How did this guy know so much about me — my name, my one night stand, ever who my wife ~~was~~ *

He stared at me and smiled, "I know what you're thinking William. I'd be thinking the same thing in your position."

"What?"

"I need your help, but first ~~let~~ tell me what you desire the most."

Tears were welling in my eyes, and I told him, even though I was sure he knew already, "I want to wake up with Hannah's face on the pillow next to mine. I want to be able to watch my son grow up, to take him to a game or two, —" I blurted.

"What if I was ~~to~~ ~~make~~ do this for you. Would you help me then?"

It was crazy talk, how could this man possibly get me back together with my wife and child. But it all seemed

perfectly logical somehow, it was certainly more believable a
what he told me next. I nodded yes to his question

"But how can I help you?"

He closed those ocean-blue eyes and steepled his
fingers. Then he gulped the scotch in one fluid motion.

"What I'm about to tell you, only a handful of
people have ever known. And those few only came
managed to remain sane. , I'm not what I appear
to be..."

His story was an impossible one. I sat there as
he told me of the Controllers: Beings who existed on a different
plane, to ours. Watching us, keeping records and manipulating
us from behind the scenes. And he, this strange man
sat opposite me, used to be one of the Clan. "
clique "It's happened before," he said, " members of
an coterie have seen your existence on this planet, and
despite the misery, wars and so on, have envied your flesh
physical form.

"I don't think I understand."

He sighed - " I was tired of making the choices — deciding who lives, who
dies, who is lucky, who will never succeed. You see, over the
centuries I've developed a conscience. So I slipped through
the barrier crossed over the threshold."

The words were outlandish, and he had one hell of
an imagination. He almost had me convinced this was all real.

"You're telling me none of us have free-will, that
there's no such thing as destiny," I spat

"Oh, there is destiny alright, just not in the way
you mean."

I frowned, "And what about God?"

"What about him?" he replied then remained silent.

Finally I broke the silence "So where do I fit in?"
"Every so often a person is born; some are
you are they have trouble focussing on shall we say. Their names
such a and some, ah, basic details are stored in the vaults." If
person I can just stay with you for a short while, it might throw
million. them off my trail."

"Who?" certain
"My pursuers - members of the order at quite
proficient at tracing and capturing malcontents."

"Ah, I've had enough of this - you're such, you know
what," I shouted, "leave me out of your twisted delusions

The man bowed his head as I started away
from his table. I'd barely gone three steps when the
lights above me blinked on and off.

134

We'd had power surges (cuts and) before, but this was different. The strip lighting was winking in a uniform way, almost as if it was tapping out a message.

The few remaining customers looked up, as did Shiel - Soul stood at the far end of the bar.

I turned back to look at my mysterious friend in the booth. His head was still bowed, but I could see a bead of sweat rolling down his forehead. He said only two words (3), and they chilled me to my very core/soul.

"They've found me."

I went over to booth and grabbed the man by the arm (pulled with). He looked up at me, eyes wide - but this time in fear.

"Come on," I said, "There's a back door to this place."

I don't know what made me help - I still didn't believe his tale of omnipotent creatures * - but the man was obviously terrified, and on the run from somebody: cops, bounty hunters - I didn't know, and I didn't much care. I just wanted to get him the hell out of there.

(Playing over as the cops)

We stumbled out into the alley behind Mich's. My friend could barely walk, so I ended up half carrying him past the trash cans and litter.

It was fairly dark, the only light coming from tiny windows in the buildings above, and as we made our way down that passage I became more and more scared.

The street was about 40, maybe 60 metres away, but it might as well been 1000 - The man was getting too heavy to lift - his feet dragging on the rough concrete floor.

Then I heard a noise behind me: A kind of whizzing (fizzing) like the sound of a faulty plug makes - only louder. (Crackling and)

I turned, but I wished to god I'd just kept going. That sight froze me to the spot, making it impossible to escape.

In the alley-way, a white and blue circle had opened up out of nowhere and two figures were stepping out. It was hard to make out their details (features) because of the light from the door, but they appeared to be wearing hooded cloaks.

There was no time to run, they were on us in a heartbeat. Up close, I could see that it was no cloak they wore, but rather a thick leathery membrane (hid) their bodies and features. The same deep-blue eyes shone from their heads, but far brighter than the man's.

One reached out a hand, a gnarled twisted and rusting appendage. It clamped onto the man's shoulder with all the power of a hydraulic arm.

Though I was shaking, and about 2 seconds away from letting my bowels (have their way), I tried to ~~compulsively~~ dodge ~~both~~ between this thing and the man.

There was another flash of light ~~too~~ and suddenly I was ~~caught~~ bent double on the floor, experiencing pain the likes of which I hope you'll never know.

And the second 'controller' was stood over me — he seemed huge ~~to me~~ at the time, though he couldn't have been any taller than the average human.

~~I~~ I gaped through water-logged ~~soaked~~ eyes as he peeled back the ~~hood~~ membrane. Its ~~v~~ skin was ~~creamy~~ smooth with raised pink veins criss-crossing over the face. Like the man, its cheeks bulged out and ~~it~~ it ~~was~~ was almost ~~there~~ bald. But there was no trace of white in its eyes — only the blue staring, staring at me. I felt as though ~~they~~ were going to set me alight.

"No, ~~stop~~!" cried the man from behind it, "I'll go with you!"

And then it floated It ~~stared~~ ~~looked~~ looked at the man, then at me; — ~~and~~ ~~floated~~ away, ~~without~~ back to ~~his~~ its colleague.

~~and~~ The pair hooked my friend under the arms and carried him back to the burning sphere. I couldn't move, let alone shout out for help —— But as they disappeared through the hole, I heard the man's voice in my head

"Don't worry William, I keep my promises."

Then I must have passed out because all ~~e~~ I can remember is blackness.

It wasn't until a day or so later that I found out what he meant. Hannah and Benjamin turned up at my flat ~~and~~ unexpectedly. She wanted to give it another go. I was, understandably, thrilled at the time.

But the events of that night have left a stain on my soul. The knowledge that this is all pointless, that whatever decision we make, whatever choice — even if its only say, ~~what you'll~~ ~~whether~~ for dinner that night — is preordained and not really your decision at all — ~~it~~ weighs on my mind. How could it not.

Now I know ~~that~~ ~~the~~ controllers exist, I can think of nothing ~~no~~ else, and my once happy life seems so hollow.

And what of the man they took ~~away~~ back with them? What was his fate? With all our flaws he still envied us, though I can't think why (as I can't seem to sleep much nowadays)

I watch for him at night, hoping he'll come back to

136

tell me it was all a dream, but deep down I know that will never happen.

And there one other thing I know as well, don't ask me how, or why, I just know. One day the controllers I'll meet again, maybe here, maybe in their world, but it will happen.

And maybe one day on that we'll the human race gain back their freedom.

Until then, I can only watch and wait...

Handwritten Corrections to 'The Controllers'/'The Secret'/'Secrets' on Original Typed Manuscript (circa 1997)

Secret

The ~~Customer~~

(A Controllers Story)

I could tell as soon as he walked through the door that he wasn't your average frequenter of Mick's place.

For a start he wore a suit. Sure, it was tattered, and scuffed at the sleeves, but it was a suit all the same. And his black shoes looked like they'd been shiny at one time or another.

But the man himself, well that was a different matter. Deathly pale skin was stretched tight over his face, especially at the cheekbones - which threatened to break through at any moment - and what little hair he had was slicked back; plastered to his ~~rounded~~ scalp. *yet*

And those eyes! I swear when he looked round the room you could feel shivers going down the spines of the regulars - those who were still sober at that time of night, anyway.

Then his intense gaze settled on me behind the bar. I felt him drilling into my head with those piercing blue orbs, wielded with all the skill of a trained hypnotist. I tried to look away, but found myself loosing the battle of wills.

In the end it was the man who broke off the connection. He approached the bar - quick strides at first, then gradually slowing as he reached his destination. He placed a bony hand on the counter, leaning against it for support. I remember thinking he'd probably fall down if that crutch was removed.

Shirl, over at the far end, kept her distance. She had no intentions of coming near, let alone serving this guy. I couldn't say I really blamed her.

Yet something about him fascinated me, don't ask what or why. Finally I plucked up the courage to speak.

'What'll it be?' I said quietly.

He looked at me and replied in a strong, deep voice that betrayed no hint of a discernible accent, 'Scotch. Bring it over to the corner booth.'

With that he left a crumpled bill on the bar and headed for his table.

My palms were sweating as I fixed his drink. When he slid onto the green leather bench, I heard his bones crack like shots from a rifle.

He stared at me again as I brought the Scotch over.

'There you go. Is that all you want?'

He nodded.

done - ~~typed~~

138

'Okay, well enjoy your drink then.' I was just about to turn when he grabbed my arm. I was so startled, I nearly dropped my tray.

'Sit down,' he whispered.

'Really, I can't. I'm working-'

He said the words again, 'Sit down.' There was no threat in his invitation and the grip wasn't particularly strong, with those frail hands, how could it be? but I obeyed his order all the same. Maybe it was those eyes; maybe he *was* a hypnotist of some kind, I thought.

But the bar was pretty slow that Thursday, and Shirl could handle any new customers that might drift in. I figured, what's the harm?

He still had hold of my wrist, and I could feel him fingering the skin for a pulse. He closed his eyes a fraction, still looking at me through the slits. Then a chilling smile swept across his face, and he let go.

'You are someone with a great deal on his mind,' he said matter of factly.

'How did you-?'

'I am very perceptive. Perhaps you would like to tell me about your wife and child?'

I hesitated, the words throwing me completely, 'I-I don't know what you're talking about.'

'Yes you do. They left you, didn't they?'

It wasn't possible for him to know these things, unless... 'Did Hannah send you? Where is she, please I have to-'

'Calm yourself,' he said, 'I have never met your wife. I am merely an...interested party.'

'A lawyer?' I was angry, yet something was keeping me in check, rooting me to the spot.

'No. I am here to help you.'

I don't know why, maybe it was something in this angry guy's voice, but I believed him. When he asked me again to tell him about my troubles, I complied instantly.

139

'I don't know how it got so out of hand. We were fine, you know. Everything was great until I screwed it all up. I thought I'd got it under control, the gambling. I kept telling myself one more and I'll come –'

He laughed out loud at this remark, as if he knew something I didn't. 'Please continue.'

'Well, when Hannah found out, she went crazy. We'd already been having problems, I guess this topped it off. She left last Saturday taking Danny with her. I haven't heard from them since.'

The Stranger leant forwards, 'So tell me, what do you desire most in the world?'

'What?' His question came out of nowhere, and I was caught slightly off guard.

'I asked what you would like most in the world.'

I had a feeling he already knew (he seemed to know everything else) but I told him anyway, 'Okay, I want a chance to prove that I can change, make a fresh start. I'll do anything to get them back.'

His smile was twisted, 'Good, good. Now, what if I told you there was a way to do this? That I could arrange it?'

It was my turn to laugh rivulets of salt water dripping into my mouth. It was impossible. How could this bizarre excuse of a man possibly fix my life? All the same, curiosity got the better of me and I heard him out.

'I know what you are thinking, but I *can* help you. But only if you help me.'

There was an authority in his dialogue, the patter of a master manipulator or con artist, but for once in my life I dared to hope, 'What can I do?'

He gulped the Scotch greedily; a trickle broke free and ran down his chin. Then he steepled his fingers and began.

'What I am about to tell you, only a handful of people have ever known. And of that handful, only two retained their sanity once they were "enlightened". Shall I go on?'

I nodded vaguely, not really understanding what he meant, but desperate to know his big secret.

'Then understand this: I am not what I appear to be...'

His story was an unbelievable one: a joke told with the straightest of faces. I sat there as he informed me that there were beings beyond my understanding who exist on a plane to the left of our world, watching us, keeping records and regulating mankind from behind the scenes.

And he, this strange man who sat opposite me, had been one of the clan.

'It has happened before,' he said in hushed tones, 'Members of our clique have spoken out about the intense misery we caused your race: wars, disease, prejudice...all were our doing. They were the few who developed a conscience over time. They grew weary of deciding who lived, who died, who suceeded and who failed. But they were quickly silenced. Only one or two dared breach the barrier and escape.'

'Where to?'

'Here, of course,' he paused, more for dramatic effect than anything, I presumed, 'Some went to ground and have never been heard of since. Others were not so fortunate.'

At first I thought this man was quite clearly insane. But he had one hell of an imagination, and I began to get drawn into the tale. Again I wondered if it was his eyes, because he never took them off me once throughout his little performance. Anyway, I decided to play along with him for the time being.

'So where to from? — What do you want from me?' ~~far from~~

He smiled that terrifying, all-knowing smile once more, the grin of a teacher who has all the answers in a particularly hard exam. 'It will all become clear in time, but first we must go. ~~Now, quickly, before it is too late.~~' It is / not safe here

He obviously believed what he was saying, but the rational side of my brain was finally waking up. And after that, my patience wore thin pretty quickly, 'I'm not goin anywhere. I've listened to what you had to say, but quite frankly I think you need serious psychiatric...

'I know it is hard, but what I have told you is the truth. You have to believe me,' he pleaded.

'I'm sorry, I've got a bar to run.'

The man sighed and bowed his head as I walked away from the table.

I'd barely gone three steps when the lights above blinked on and off. Now, we'd had plenty of power surges before, but ~~we~~ at Mich's this was something else. The fluorescent panels were winking in a uniform way, almost as if they were tapping out a message in Morse code.

The remaining customers reared their heads, as did Shirl - who hadn't moved from the other end of the bar.

I turned round to look at my mysterious acquaintance in the booth. His head was still bowed and I could see a bead of sweat trailing down his temple. He said only four words. They were enough.

'I have been found.'

I rushed back to join him, and when I touched his shoulder, the man jumped slightly. He stared up at me, eyes wide with panic - blood vessels throbbing in the corners.

'Come on,' I said, 'There's a back door to this place.' story

I don't know what made me help. I hadn't changed my mind about his tale of omnipotent creatures (who played with us like dolls in a Wendy house) or the deal he'd talked about if I went with him. But the man was obviously terrified of somebody, or something. I couldn't just stand idly by, even if he was a ~~madman~~. crackpot I'm sure it's these kind.

the more I listened the more

you must really hurt yourself

Handwritten Corrections to 'Eye of the Beholder' on Original Typed Manuscript (circa 2000/2001)

<u>Eye of the Beholder</u>

The *Beholder* is ageless.

Since time immemorial, it has resided at the core of its world. At the centre. The junction. Enormous and blue, a great eye with veins snaking from its side, outstretching into the vastness beyond.

And it sees everything. Absolutely everything.

Occasionally it feels the souls trapped beneath its thin, diaphanous outer-layer, struggling to escape. (Like floaters in any ordinary eyeball.) They push up towards the surface, sensing that if they could only break through this barrier they would be free. But each time they come too near, the *Beholder* would blink, pulling its dark eyelid over the top and dispersing them, clearing its vision. Their anguish empowered it, juiced the world above and enabled the fundamental work to continue.

And now, as was its want, the *Beholder* allows itself to rise mentally through the blanket of dirt that keeps it hidden, and safe. It gazes upon the many cities that make up its world, surrounded by a strange mist that sets it apart from the rest of reality. It watches the autochthonous volcanoes belch forth their cold, anaemic fire, and observes the figures flitting about in the dark streets below. Secret, hooded beings that band together in twos and threes. Its children and its protectors. Hurrying, they make their way along the Byzantine patchwork of gitties and gennels, along winding roads and down twisting alleyways; their incantations spoken without words. The *Beholder* goes with them all, following each one individually to its destination - in the spear-shaped living towers that they called their homes.

Each hooded figure has its own niche in the minarets, its own niche, hollowed-out bowers they can claim as their own: where the organic framework of the steeple's interior will respond to their singular wishes and demands. Seats instinctively ... up for them to sit at, growing out of the floor, and the perfectly clear globes they use to view and "control" customarily leap out from the walls to congregate about them, each one displaying images from another place, *another world*. A blue-white planet they have no name for, but which the natives insist upon calling Earth.

It intrigued the *Beholder* to see where they came from, the spirits ... inside its own innards. Where they began and ended. One of its children bent forwards, an almost turquoise glow radiating from beneath its fleshy cowl. The *Beholder* knew that under the hood (itself a functioning part of the ..., a protective second skin) its face was a map of bone, held in check by a tight, mottled, and hairless covering of flesh. And in the middle was a single cerulean eye not unlike its own. Indeed, it was the *Beholder*'s gift to them. A miniature representation of itself they carried about with them everywhere. The key to their power.

And their inheritance.

The *Beholder* watched as its ancillary watched. A life just beginning on the "screen". White liquid gushing out, containing millions and millions of tiny life forms. It observed as they swam upstream, fighting against the tide. One survivor. The choice was made (indeed, it had been made before they ...) made it to the finish line. And yet there could be only one winner in this race. The winner butted its way inside, leaving its companions to perish on the outskirts. The egg was fertilised and prepared to be nurtured to size. Would it be twins or perhaps malformed? No, not this time. The embryo developed normally, by fourteen weeks limbs and internal organs in place, and now all that remained was growth. Any one of a billion things could have gone wrong during the course of the pregnancy both outside and in. But they didn't. It was routine in every way, apart from the mother experiencing a touch of heartburn now and again (only a sign that it had a full head of hair according to old wive's tales) and an aching back. The small human being ... comfortable and warm in amniotic fluid for a little over nine months. The most peaceful and content it would ever feel in its entire life.

And there followed an easy birth as well. No Herculean labour or caesarean section. Let it come naturally; the time for sorrow would soon find her (as now the *Beholder* came to think of it as a girl - a baby girl called Lucy). The *Beholder* scrutinised, but never interfered. That was not its intent, nor its purpose. It left that to the creatures inhabiting this domain.

Maybe cot death might claim her, is that what its progeny had in mind? No, it would let her live...for now. The first real scare would be the illness that came like an amateur assassin in the night, serious enough to warrant several days back in hospital. Thank God her parents had found her in time, barely breathing. No, not God. The *Beholder* knew whom they should really be thanking. For not only was the hooded one directing the life of this child (its long, ashen fingers stabbing the air, provoking incidents) but also that of its parents as well, adding more worry to their day-to-day existences, encouraging them not to have any more children.

But how glad they'd been when their Lucy was released, able now to celebrate her second birthday - while all the time, in the back of their minds, they wondered whether it would happen again. Whether she'd be taken from them one day.

Not yet...There was still much to do.

The daughter grew, filling out her new body, muscles strengthening, bones developing with each intake of calcium, hair turning from blonde to brown and spreading down past her shoulders.

The world was a fantastic place, Lucy learnt. Beautiful, colourful and bright. But it could also be a place of anger and insecurity. Of agony and tears. Too many close calls to recount: the time she put her hand out to stroke a relative's puppy and it bit her, tiny needle-teeth puncturing her skin, acquainting her with blood for the first time; falling off the swing in her back garden and grazing her knee on the hard ground; a drink of water going down the wrong way and taking her breath for a moment; the sensation of touching a fireguard and burning her fingers - no, Lucy hadn't liked that at all. And the memory of being shouted at for opening the gates and nearly making it to the roadside (oh, but the cars were so, so pretty...), her dad's face turning so red she thought it might explode.

School presented Lucy with a whole new set of problems, for although she was fairly quick to learn, one of the older teachers took an immediate and vehement dislike to her. She would later learn it was because of some trick her father had played when he had attended the school. Lucy found herself being punished for things she hadn't done. It was always *her* talking in class, even though she was paying complete attention to the teacher's oration. Basically it was a mess. No one was happy, not the teacher, not the pupil and certainly not her parents, who demanded to know why their little girl came home crying four out of five nights a week.

Finally it all came out one evening and, after a blazing row down at the school, which the headmistress defended the member of staff in question to the hilt, their daughter was moved to another educational facility. Already behind with her studies because of the trouble at home and at the school, Lucy was forced to catch up with the others, which to her credit she did admirably. However, this reputation as a trouble-shaker stuck with her, and she was never really given the opportunity to show what she could do - left out of sports teams and school plays purposely (she felt). It followed her right up to secondary school, where she found herself the target for bullies because of her miserable disposition - unaware as they were that ever since her menstrual cycle had started to turn, she'd suffered from terrible bouts of depression.

On one occasion they'd waited for Lucy to begin the walk to the bus stop after school and dragged her behind a hedge. Careful not to leave any incriminating marks on her, they pinned her to the floor and forced her to eat dirt and grass, then stole her bag with her books, homework and purse inside. She'd learnt her lesson, though, and told her parents she'd mislaid it (for which she was grounded until the end of term).

This is not to say that Lucy didn't make any friends. She did. And to those who openly sought her friendship, she gave one-hundred-percent loyalty. But then along came boys and she was soon forgotten about as her mates – once the most ardent men-haters you ever did see – chose to spend all their time with members of the opposite sex. Given half a chance Lucy might have joined them, but her self-esteem had never been up to much and those pictures in magazines or on TV didn't help either, celebrating the statuesque figure of the supermodel or the voluptuous curves of a page-three girl. All she saw when she looked in the mirror was a Plain Jane with braces on her teeth and spots on her face.

So Lucy chose to devote herself to her studies instead, gearing herself up for the big exams she'd take at the end of the school year. Exams that would be her key to bigger and better things (she loved writing and pictured herself one day working in a newspaper office - if her grades were good enough, that is).

143

Unfortunately her parents chose that particular time to break up; well, you could hardly blame them after her father found out mother had been seeing a younger man while he was at work – a man who lived across the road from them (the subject of many a young girl's daydream – including Lucy's). Her mother left with the youth to go and live ten miles away in a small rented flat, the aftermath of a particularly nasty row which her father had even raised his fist though never followed through.

Her emotions all over the place, Lucy screwed up just about every single exam. Words like extenuating circumstances were bandied about, but the long and the short of it was she'd have to re-sit if she wanted to get anywhere. She opted instead to leave school with a D in Physics and Maths, and an E in English, drawing dole for almost a year while she got her 'head together'. Comfort eating became her biggest weakness, sat watching soaps and talk shows on daytime TV (possibly where the notion came from in the first place). Later she'd bring it all up in the bathroom, just in time to greet her father home from a hard day's work at the car plant.

He encouraged her to get out more, pass more time with people her own age. So she did. Her weekends were spent in town, where she discovered a whole other scene and got hooked up with some very dodgy characters. But for once in her life she felt she belonged. She got invited to some extremely private parties and indulged herself freely, the comfort eating being replaced by more hazardous pursuits. It was at one such gathering that she met her first boyfriend. He called himself Ziggy (it wasn't his real name, he just used it because he thought he looked like a famous singer – or maybe it was because he didn't want anyone knowing his true identity) and she thought he was "the one".

'You're really gorgeous, you know,' he used to tell her, before sticking his hand up her jumper and fumbling around with her on a bed that wasn't even theirs. And it was more or less true; Lucy was quite attractive now that the braces and acne had gone. But she soon found out Ziggy was sleeping around with most of the women she considered friends, telling them all the same thing before pouncing. To get back at him, Lucy did the same: parading a string of faceless males in front of him and bedding them all with a mixture of glee and regret.

The warped dream of her late teens came to a shocking conclusion, though, when one of the guests at a party choked on his own vomit after foolishly mixing spirits and hard-core drugs. An ambulance was called and the police weren't far behind, detaining some and arresting others – including Ziggy (real name Keith Hedges) who it turned out was a pretty proficient dealer in his spare time. The jolt of being questioned by the police, not to mention seeing that guy's corpse on the floor of the bathroom – spittle and dried sick forming a halo around his head – was enough to snap her out her reverie.

Lucy's dad, summoned to pick her up from the station (no charges this time, just a caution), wasn't as angry as she thought he'd be. He just seemed tired and so old that day. He helped her get over the addictions she'd picked up the best way he knew how, with love and support, and for that she would always be grateful to him.

Eventually she got her life back on track, snaring herself a job at a pet-shop. In spite of her long-standing fear of dogs, and saving up her money as she was blowing it all on cheap thrills. She made new friends, better friends and started to enjoy herself more and more. In her early twenties she'd experience some of the best times she was ever likely to know. This included meeting Greg, the pet-shop owner's son, who arrived home from his lengthy gap-year travels back one day and bumped into her – literally – as she entered the shop.

'Sorry,' he said, helping her pick up the bags of bird nuts she'd been carrying. And that was that. The next thing she knew they were dating, real dates – not the wham-bams she was used to. This was love, no doubt about it, and it certainly put her fling with Ziggy into perspective.

Then came the next scene. There was this disease, she'd read about it in all the papers, seen it on the news. And it wasn't just confined to the gay community as the experts had first thought. No, this plague had spread outwards and apparently you could catch it from sharing needles or from having sex without protection. And this disease could kill you – stone dead. Lucy thought about the many men at those parties, the drugs available... Weeks, months of agonising, of keeping Greg at arm's length. Should she tell him of her past and risk losing everything they had together? Would he understand if she went to be tested? Would he ever trust her again?

It was so humiliating, confessing all, but as it turned out she had nothing to worry about. Their relationship (and Greg) was much stronger than that. He even went with her and took a test himself. But then there was more waiting, more doubts, more recriminations, before they finally discovered they were both clean.

They'd only been sleeping together a few months when she skipped a period. For the first time Lucy missed the all-encompassing gloom that arrived and settled in for one week out of every four; indeed, she urged it to come, because at least then she'd know she wasn't... But how could she be? They'd taken precautions (after what she'd been through she'd insisted)...The injustice of it, after all those years of...for it to happen now that she'd found someone...someone truly special.

More sleepless nights. Building up to telling Greg again. She'd wanted to do it the day she found out, but he'd been so full of his own good news: a brand new job working on promotions for the football club, with more importantly, decent rates of pay. She didn't want to bring him down.

The time came when she had to say something, before it was too late – regardless of the fact she'd already decided to keep the baby. Much to her relief he was delighted and asked her if she wanted to get a place together. She hated leaving her dad after everything he'd done, but he understood and was happy for them (her mother, likewise, now living on her own after the plumber cut out on her). So they set up home, Lucy and Greg, and she enjoyed every minute of it: choosing furniture for their small - cosy bungalow; arranging colour schemes; getting everything just right. It made up for the terrible bouts of morning sickness. Greg's father gave her plenty of time off from the shop, after all it was *his* grandchild she was carrying.

They settled into a routine, and although it was never spoken out loud, both of them knew that the next stage in their relationship would probably be marriage – perhaps once the baby was born.

The accident came right out of the blue. Greg was on his way to ground to sort out publicity for a league match, when the train he was on derailed. It wasn't the worst catastrophe the rail service had suffered, in fact they were lucky more people hadn't been killed (or so the TV newsman had announced that night) – seventeen injured, mostly just minor cuts and bruises.

Three dead.

Lucy remembered Greg kissing her on the forehead that morning before leaving, then placing a hand on her stomach.

'Take care of kiddo,' he'd said, smiling as he used the baby's nickname.

'I will,' she replied.

They were the last words ever to pass between them.

The severe torment of grief, the agony of loss. What was the purpose? Out on the streets were rapists, muggers, killers...roaming free, healthy and...and the nicest man to ever walk...he was...

The months following the funeral were devastating. Lucy couldn't afford to keep up payments on the bungalow, and so she moved out. It wasn't as if she wanted to stay there now anyway – it had been their place meant for a couple...a family.

She moved back in with her dad, accepting financial help from Greg's parents. Lucy's mum came back to see her, to be with her child in her time of need, and ended up staying permanently, making it up with her estranged husband after all these years. They guided her through the last stages of her pregnancy, and were there at the hospital as she endured a staggering nineteen-hour labour (the doctors almost lost Lucy twice) the product of which was Annabel, a healthy seven-pound baby girl.

After that, her daughter took priority. She was too busy to think about her heartache, except on off days or in the moments just before dawn.

Life goes on, she'd tell herself. And indeed it did, for her, for little Annabel, and for her parents, who now seemed more in love than they'd ever been before.

She went through the highs and lows of bringing up a child as a single parent, with friends and family around her. Lucy just about coped. She hadn't been looking for more complications in her life, but just as before fate (if she only knew) pushed her in a certain direction and she met Robin in the supermarket one day. At first she wasn't sure, not this soon after Greg; but she couldn't help how she felt about him, and it was blatantly obvious he felt the same way.

Lucy worried about introducing him to Annabel, now five going on forty-five. But the pair hit it off straight away. Her parents applauded Lucy's choice (a handsome banker with a house and a charming disposition) and even Greg's family gave her their blessing, once she assured them they would never have cause to feel left out.

This time Lucy did marry, and she had another baby. A son, which she insisted they call Greg, and not many men would have been okay with that, but Robin was. Once again Lucy experienced a period of joy (not total joy, for can such a thing ever exist? but close enough to be mistaken for it without further examination). Lucy was even looking into home study courses, finally retaking her exams before attempting a degree the same way. Maybe she hadn't left it too late after all, and that job as a journalist was out there somewhere, just waiting for her.

Then came the night of the fire.

Robin was out of town for the weekend. Annabel was at her grandparents (on Greg's side), while Lucy and little Greg were back at the homestead enjoying their quality mother-son time together.

Some time between two and three o'clock in the morning – or so the investigators said – there was an electrical surge in the kitchen that caused the fridge's plug to catch light, sparks from which ignited the writing pad on the kitchen top bearing a list of groceries for that week's shopping trip. The fire then took hold, fuelled by the wood-effect cupboards and the kitchen blinds. Within minutes the tiles on the floor were melting and the hallway carpet was ablaze. Smoke set off the fire alarm but the battery was flat and it only managed a few strangled beeps before retiring. Lucy began to cough as the tendrils of smog rose and entered her room, seeping under the door. She woke up and understood what was happening immediately and called the emergency services using the bedside phone.

Then, staggering onto the landing, she found herself ignified by a thick, black cloud. Lucy fought to reach Greg's room and gathered up the half-conscious toddler in her arms. She made for the window, but realised that the fifteen-foot drop into the garden was too big a risk to take. Their only option was to go downstairs and get out through the front door.

Barking like a dog as the smoke took its toll, Lucy wrapped her boy in a blanket and ran back out onto this landing. She aimed for the staircase. Lucy its vague outline barely discernible in the smoke. The floor creaked and the heat from below scolded her bare feet through the boards. Lucy reached the first step and, using the wall as a guide, began to descend. A tongue of fire lapped at them from the hall, through the banister's rail. Lucy kept her head down, hugging her son to her breast. She was almost at the bottom when the staircase gave way, taking Lucy into the hall.

Lucy screamed as the fire bit into her, but she rolled onto her front; the fear of crushing Greg outweighed by the terrible danger the fire posed. It fused her nightdress to her back, set her hair alight and robbed her arms of skin. Her feet and legs bubbled with the intensity of the flames, making it impossible to even crawl. The pain was unlike anything she'd ever imagined, let alone experienced, but it soon reached a crescendo and Lucy's whole body seemed to go numb. She lay there. They thought she heard noises at one point, a banging maybe: it was hard to tell above the roaring of the fire. She tried to look through dried up eyes. The front door...There was hope after all.

But it was far too late. Lucy's consciousness was ebbing away, even as the axe forced its way through the wood. Even as the men were wearing breathing apparatus broke in and located her, dragging her out to the premature applause of the crowds on the street. She woke up just once after that, as they were loading her into the ambulance. She wanted to speak, to ask about little Greg, but her voice eluded her. So instead she just looked up at the paramedic, trying to communicate her question telepathically. The axe was too busy trying to stabilise her to notice.

'Looks like full thickness...seventy, maybe eighty percent...' Lucy heard her say. Nothing about her son, though.

'How's the kid?' somebody else asked.

'He's alive.'

And as soon as she heard this, Lucy slipped quietly away. She would never know what happened after that: the fact that little Greg would have breathing problems because of his youth and early adulthood because of that night; that Robin was called back from his trip (from his mistress's bed in actual fact) to identify his wife's body, and then lived the rest of his life wracked with shame about where he'd been when the fire broke out; that Annabel would wish she'd been there that night, too, and wonder if things might have been different if she had been, that this trauma would finally impress on the stroke which had been waiting to attack her face for years and rob her another world forever over the loss of her only baby.

A baby born just yesterday in the magic than some.

There and a half decades of life, her existence making a mark, her tale intertwined with, and affecting, so than others – for her memory...

There's Lucy's story ended (an average story, more magic than some. Less so than others – no child abuse, no poverty, no prison, no deformities). Three and a half decades of life, her existence making a mark, her tale intertwined with, and affecting, so many more. But it was only a blink of an eye for the Beholder.

It drew her now into its bowels, to join the infinite number of souls confined there. Briefly it wondered who she would think when she learned the truth, the reason why she'd been born, why she'd died. And it wondered how she'd react when she knew the whole of that existence had been compelled by the hooded one with the globe, every action, every event, every decision. That as the wave of withered finger she might never have been born, conversely, lived to a ripe old age in a retirement home incapable of going to the toilet without assistance. In the end it didn't really matter. She'd served her purpose adequately. That was the important thing.

The Beholder knew that its own child would now turn its attention to another beginning, another seed and egg. Another Lucy. (No, there would never be another Lucy. It recognized that, at least.

And for its own part the great eye would watch and wait, but never interfere. For that was not its intent, not its purpose.

It felt that to the creatures inhabiting this domain ...

Original Controllers Sketches by Paul Kane (circa 1997/8)

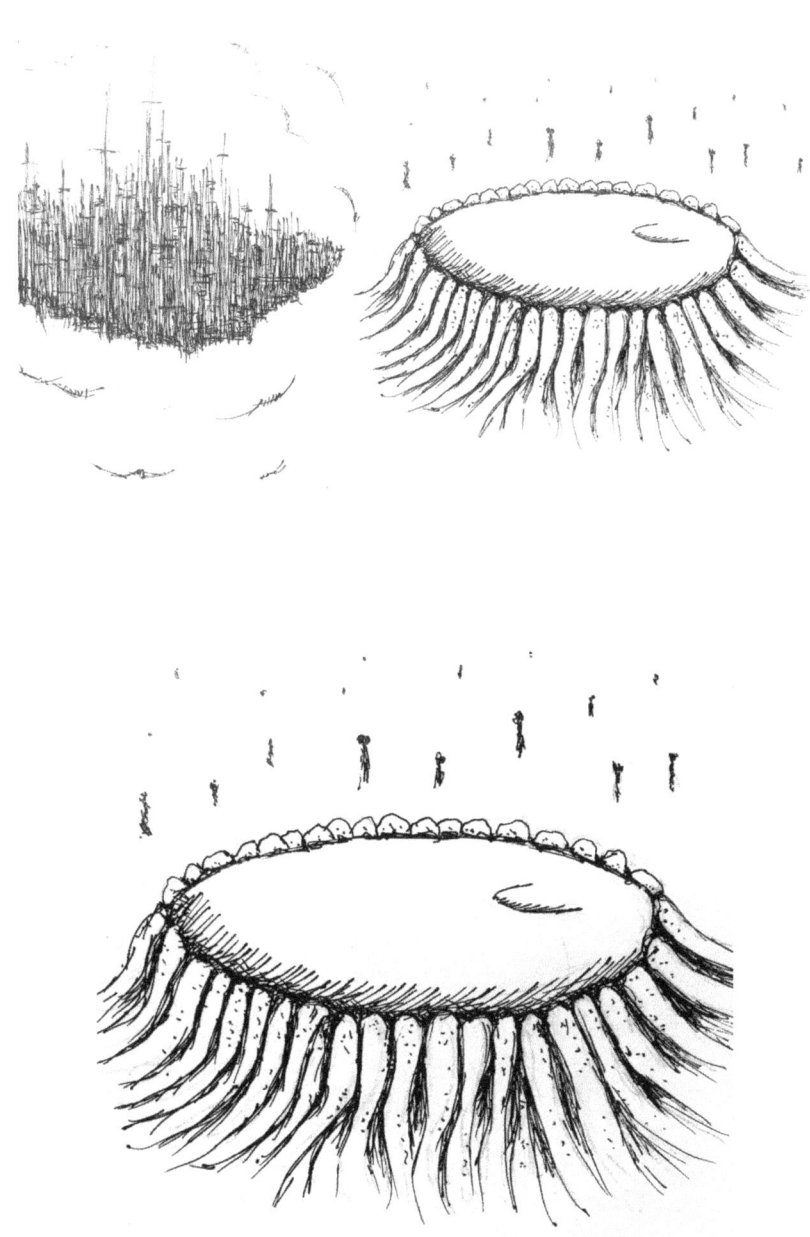

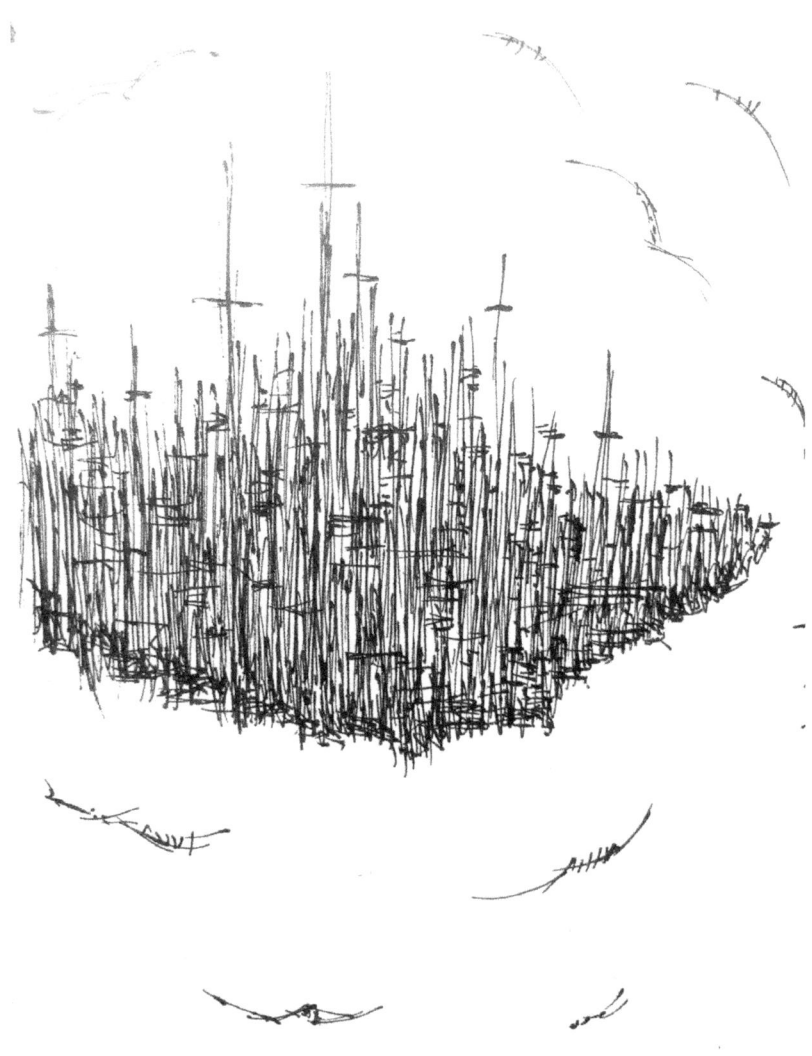

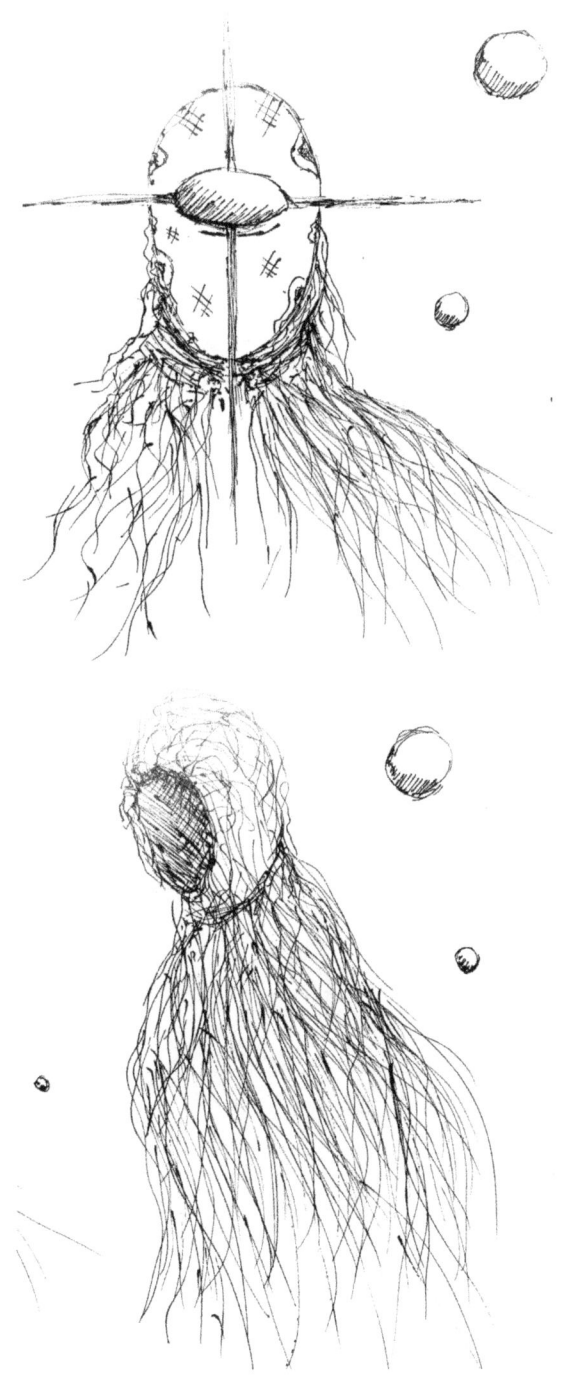

'Eye of the *Beholder*' Painting to Accompany the Story in *Alone (In the Dark)* by Paul Kane (circa 2000)

'Cubist Controllers' by Paul Kane (circa 2001)

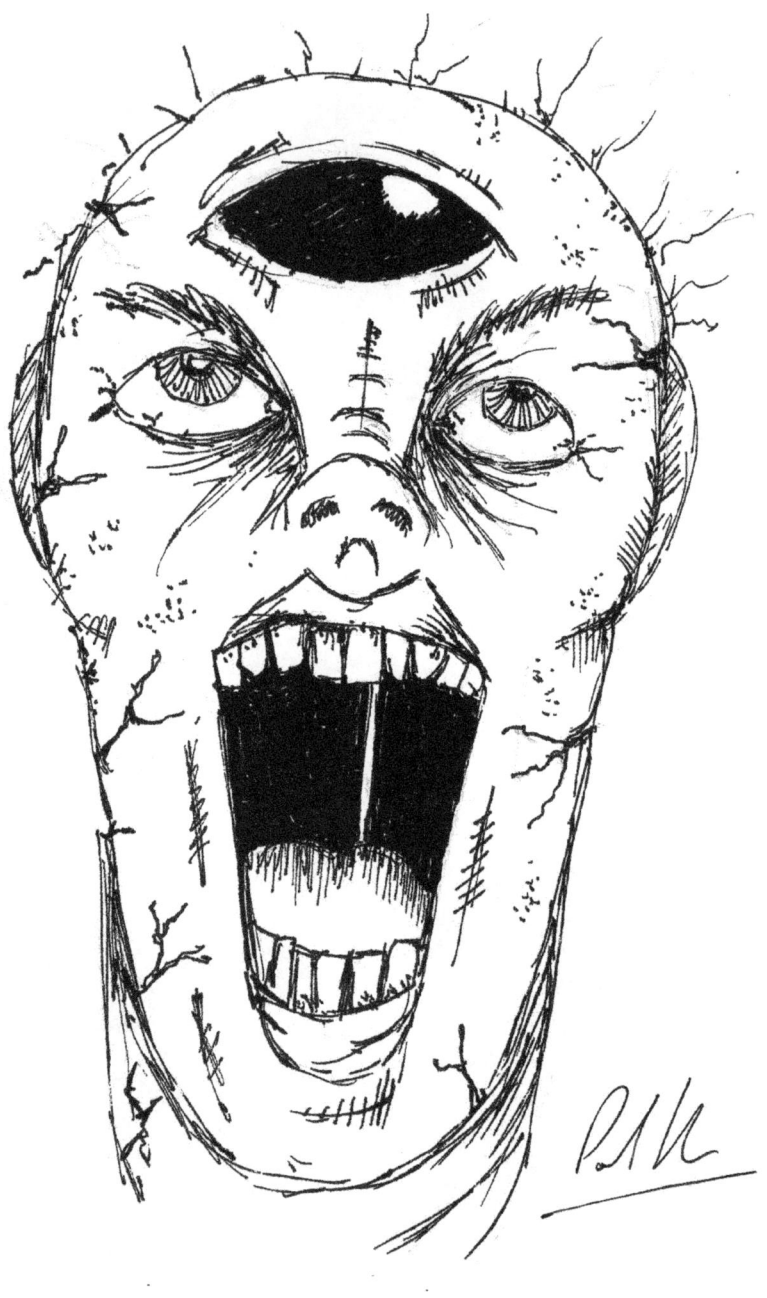

'Astral' by Steve Lines. Originally Published in *The Derelict of Death and Other Stories* (Rainfall Books, 2003)

Cover for *Pain Cages* (Books of the Dead, 2011) by Daniele Serra

Cover for *Disexistence* (Cycatrix Press, 2017) by Zach McCain

'The Controllers' by Paul Bonner Jnr (sketch and finished inks)

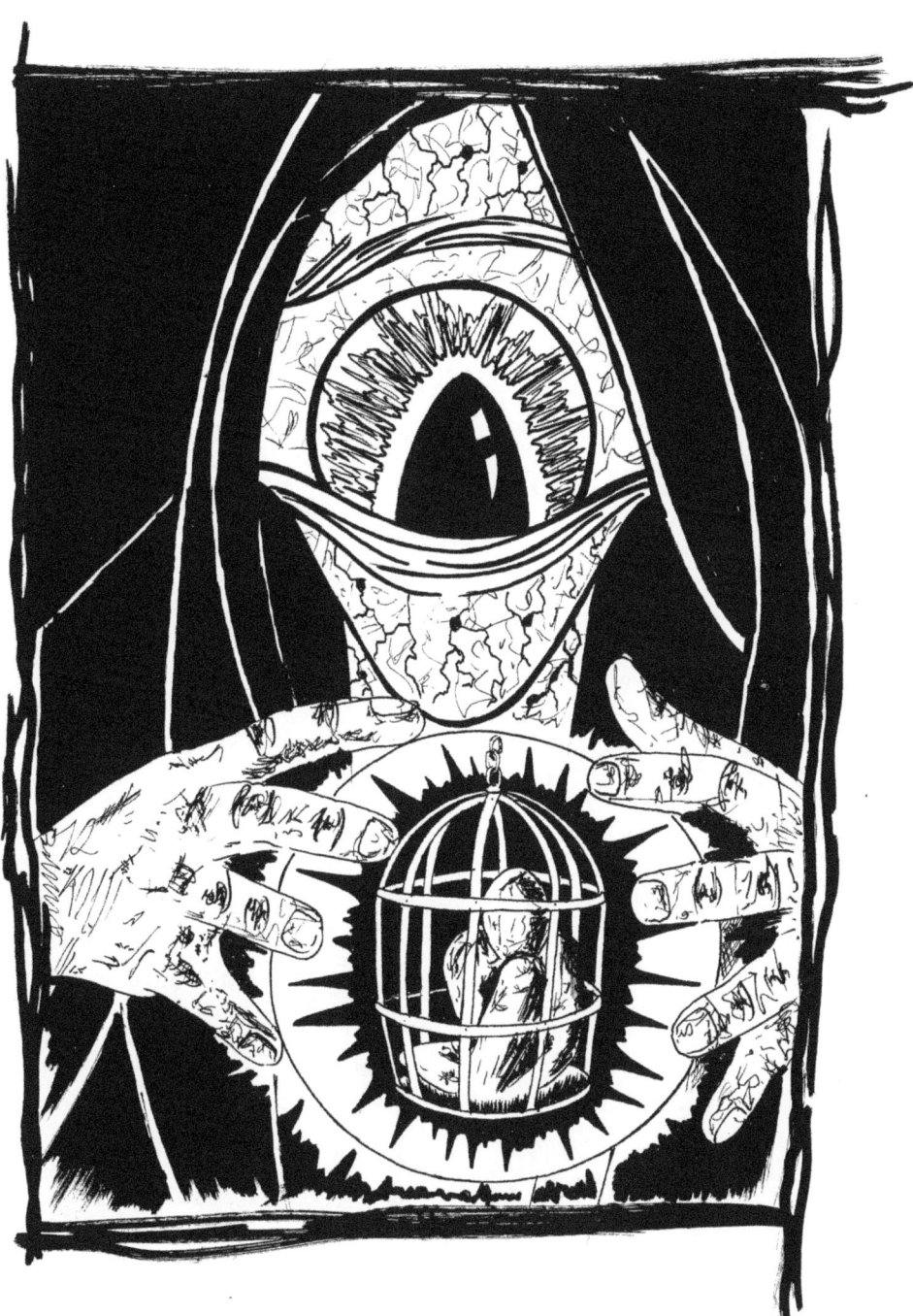

'The Controllers' by Anthony Galatis. Early Concepts and Work in progress.

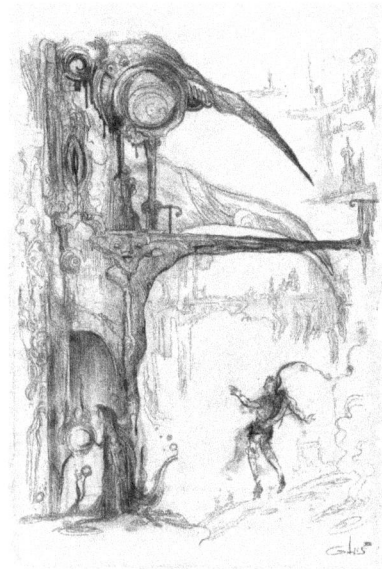

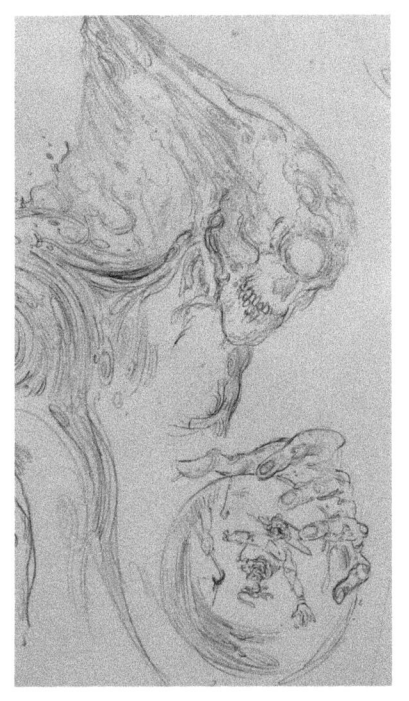

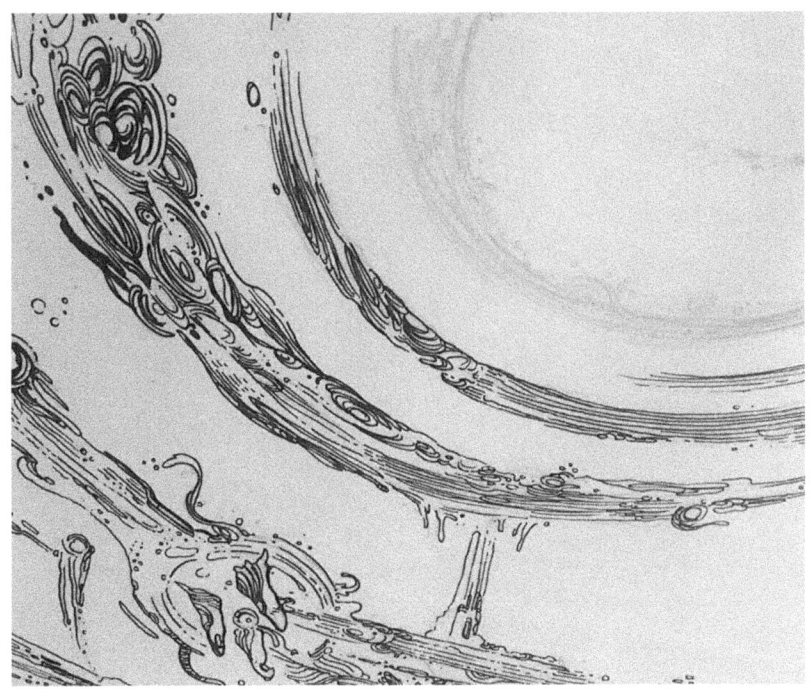

'The Controllers' by Anthony Galatis. Finished Inks.

165

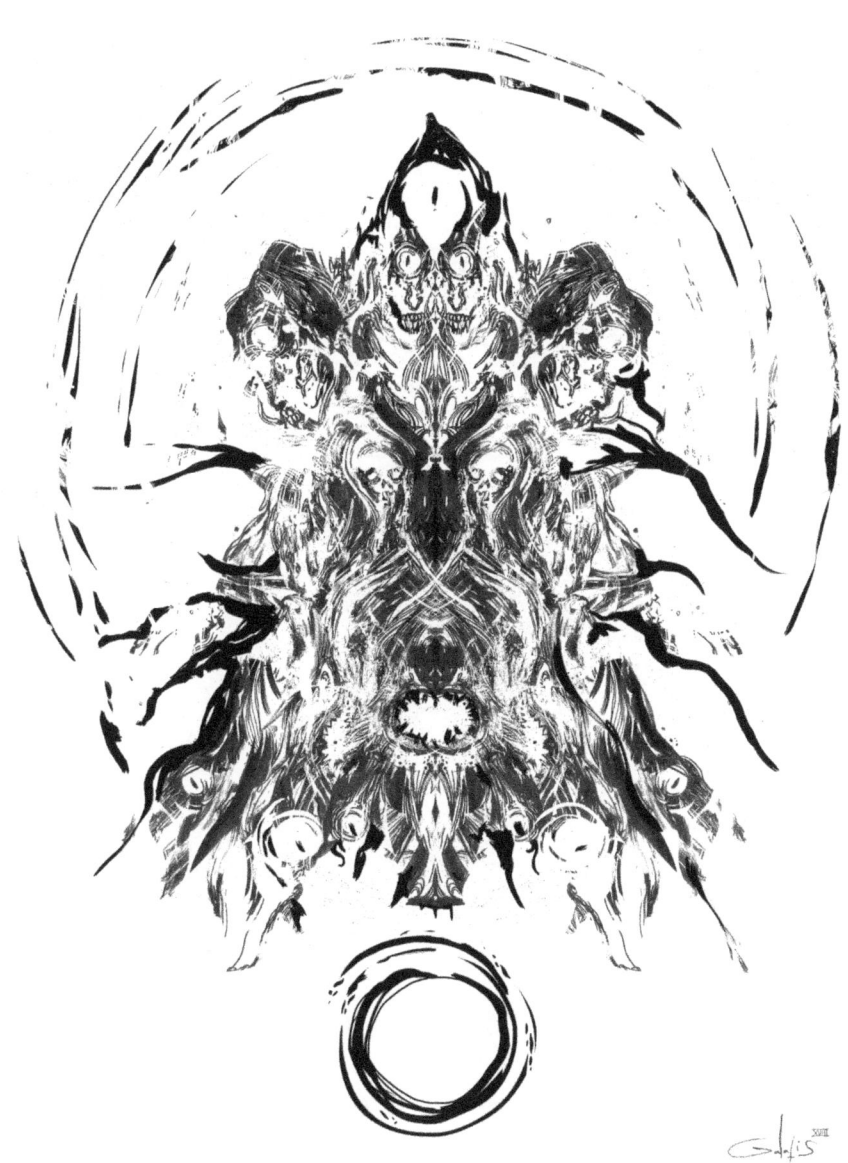

About the Author

Paul Kane is an award-winning, bestselling writer and editor based in Derbyshire, UK. His short story collections include *Alone (In the Dark), Touching the Flame, FunnyBones, Peripheral Visions, Shadow Writer, The Adventures of Dalton Quayle, The Butterfly Man and Other Stories, The Spaces Between, Ghosts*, the British Fantasy Award-nominated *Monsters, Shadow Casting, Nailbiters, Death, Disexistence, Scary Tales* and *More Monsters*. His novellas include *The Lazarus Condition, RED* and *Pain Cages* (a #1 Amazon bestseller). He is the author of such novels as *Of Darkness and Light, The Gemini Factor* and the bestselling *Arrowhead* trilogy (*Arrowhead, Broken Arrow* and *Arrowland*, gathered together in the sellout omnibus edition *Hooded Man*), a post-apocalyptic reworking of the Robin Hood mythology. His latest novels are *Lunar* (which is set to be turned into a feature film), *Sleeper(s)* (a modern, horror version of *Sleeping Beauty*), the short Y.A. novel *The Rainbow Man* (as P.B. Kane), the sequel to *RED—Blood RED*—the critically-acclaimed and award-winning *Sherlock Holmes and the Servants of Hell* from Solaris and the bestselling *Before* from Grey Matter Press.

He has also written for comics, most notably for the *Dead Roots* zombie anthology alongside writers such as James Moran (*Torchwood, Cockneys vs. Zombies*) and Jason Arnopp (*Dr Who, Friday the 13th, The Last Days of Jack Sparks*) and as part of the team turning *Clive Barker's Books of Blood* into motion comics for Seraphim/MadeFire. His stand-alone comic *The Disease*, published by Hellbound Media, was also a 2016 Ghastly Award nominated title in the 'One Shot' category. Paul is co-editor of the anthology *Hellbound Hearts* (Simon & Schuster)—stories based around the mythology that spawned *Hellraiser—The Mammoth Book of Body Horror* (Constable & Robinson/Running Press), featuring the likes of Stephen King and James Herbert, *A Carnivàle of Horror* (PS) featuring Ray Bradbury and Joe Hill, and *Beyond Rue Morgue* from Titan, stories based around Poe's detective, Dupin.

His non-fiction books include *The Hellraiser Films and Their Legacy*, *Voices in the Dark* and *Shadow Writer—The Non-Fiction. Vol. 1: Reviews* and *Vol. 2: Articles and Essays*, plus his genre journalism has appeared in the likes of *SFX*, *Fangoria*, *Dreamwatch*, *Gorezone*, *Rue Morgue* and *DeathRay*. He also co-wrote the afterword to the latest edition of Stephen King's *Night Shift* collection. He has been a Guest at Alt.Fiction five times, was a Guest at the first SFX Weekender, at Thought Bubble in 2011, Derbyshire Literary Festival and Off the Shelf in 2012, Monster Mash and Event Horizon in 2013, Edge-Lit in 2014, HorrorCon, HorrorFest and Grimm Up North in 2015, The Dublin Ghost Story Festival and Sledge-Lit in 2016, plus IMATS Olympia and Celluloid Screams in 2017, as well as being a panellist at FantasyCon and the World Fantasy Convention, and a fiction judge at the Sci-Fi London Film Festival. He is a former Special Publications Editor of the British Fantasy Society and is currently serving as co-chair for the UK arm of the Horror Writers Association.

His work has been optioned for film and television, and his zombie story 'Dead Time' was turned into an episode of the Lionsgate/NBC TV series *Fear Itself*, adapted by Steve Niles (*30 Days of Night*) and directed by Darren Lynn Bousman (*SAW II-IV*). He also scripted *The Opportunity*, which premiered at the Cannes Film Festival, *Wind Chimes* (directed by Brad 'Hallows Eve' Watson and which sold to TV), *The Weeping Woman*—filmed by award-winning director Mark Steensland, starring Tony-nominated actor Stephen Geoffreys (*Fright Night*)—and *Confidence*, directed by award-winning Mike Clarke (*A Hand to Play, Paper and Plastic*) which stars Simon Bamford (*Hellraiser, Nightbreed, Starfish*). His work for audio includes the full cast drama adaptation of *The Hellbound Heart* for Bafflegab, starring Tom Meeten (*The Ghoul*), Neve McIntosh (*Doctor Who*) and Alice Lowe (*Prevenge*), and the *Robin of Sherwood* adventure *The Red Lord* for Spiteful Puppet/ITV narrated by Ian Ogilvy (*Return of the Saint*). You can find out more at his website www.

shadow-writer.co.uk which has featured Guest Writers such as Dean Koontz, Robert Kirkman, Charlaine Harris and Guillermo del Toro.

Lightning Source UK Ltd.
Milton Keynes UK
UKHW041004190919
350012UK00010B/82/P

9 781911 143697